REMEMBER YESTERDAY

Elaine Barrington survives the car crash that kills her husband, Michael, and injures her teenaged daughter Deborah. Michael's mother, Rachel, resents the fact that Elaine survived the crash, while Deborah blames her mother for the 'careless moment', which ruined her life. Added to that, there is jealousy when mother and daughter are attracted to the same man, Andrew Nicholson. It's only when Elaine disappears that the strain she has endured is realised, and Andrew convinces Rachel and Deborah of the truth.

KATE CARTWRIGHT

REMEMBER YESTERDAY

Complete and Unabridged

LINFORD
Leicester

First published in Great Britain in 1975
by Robert Hale & Company
London

First Linford Edition
published 2008
by arrangement with
Robert Hale Limited
London

British Library CIP Data

Cartwright, Kate
　　Remember yesterday.—Large print ed.—
　　Linford romance library
　　1. Traffic accident victims—Fiction
　　2. Blame—Fiction
　　3. Mothers and daughters—Fiction
　　4. Mothers-in-law and daughters-in-law—
　　Fiction 5. Love stories 6. Large type books
　　I. Title
　　823.9'14 [F]

ISBN 978–1–84782–451–6

Published by
F. A. Thorpe (Publishing)
Anstey, Leicestershire

Set by Words & Graphics Ltd.
Anstey, Leicestershire
Printed and bound in Great Britain by
T. J. International Ltd., Padstow, Cornwall

This book is printed on acid-free paper

1

Elaine glanced at the clock again.

Her mother-in-law spoke irritably. 'I don't know why you're fidgeting. You ought to be glad that Deborah is staying at the party. Instead of coming home as soon as they've started dancing.'

Elaine didn't answer. What was there to say? Rachel Barrington always got in a jibe where she could. And who could blame her?

'I'll get your drink,' Elaine said, and got up to go to the kitchen.

'No. I'll stay up a bit longer. I want to hear how Deborah has enjoyed herself. I'll watch television. That new comedy show.'

Elaine switched on the set, then returned to her knitting. Her head ached, and she was weary. It had been a rush at the office all day, and she had done some of the housework during the evening. All she wanted now was to get her head down on a pillow. She hoped Deborah wouldn't stay out much longer.

The laughter from the comedy show was loud. Rachel was smiling at some of the jokes. Elaine closed her eyes for a moment. This was how it would always be. For the rest of her life. She would sit quietly, see that her mother-in-law had every comfort, and try to help the child who resisted every means of help. It was a long, subtle punishment.

Through the noise of the television show, a car door slammed. Elaine got up and switched off the programme without asking for Rachel's permission. They both waited for the front door to open and for the sound of Deborah's uneven step.

The heavy outer door creaked on its hinges, as if pushed by the mixture of voices — the high, excited chatter of Deborah, and the deep tones of a man. Elaine went quickly to open the sitting room door. Her daughter came in, followed by a tall man whose fair hair might have been made lighter by a sprinkling of grey, and whose face was creased by the years.

Elaine looked from one to the other.

'This is a friend of mine,' Deborah said lightly. 'Andrew Nicholson. Andrew, this is my mum. And this is my dear old gran.'

'Not so much of the 'old',' Rachel reproved fondly. 'I'm not taking to black silk and lace caps yet.'

Andrew Nicholson smiled at the two older women, then stood awkwardly.

'Sit down, Andrew,' Deborah said. 'I'll get us some coffee.' She went out to the kitchen, her limp emphasised, as it always was when she was tired. And Elaine wondered at this most unusual touch of domesticity.

'Have you known Deborah long, Mr. Nicholson?' Rachel Barrington asked the question that Elaine wanted the answer to.

'I met her this evening — at the party. She said she wanted to get home.

3

And I'd had enough, so I brought her in my car.'

'It was kind of you,' Elaine managed to say. 'I gave her the money for a taxi. She shouldn't have dragged you away.'

'I was glad of the excuse. I don't know how I got caught up with that gang of youngsters. I think Pamela's parents wanted me there to keep an eye on their property. It was Pamela Grey's party, you know.'

Elaine nodded. 'Had they — were they dancing?'

'Smooching rather than dancing. I felt too old for it, and I imagined your daughter was too young for it. So, gladly, I brought her home.'

'Well, thank you again, Mr. Nicholson,' Rachel said. 'Deborah always comes home when the dancing begins. She can't just sit and watch others. Naturally, she feels it — not being able to do the same.'

Andrew Nicholson raised his eyebrows. 'You mean because of her slight limp? That shouldn't stop her, not with

4

the stand around and wriggle brigade. It might be difficult if there were still old-fashioned waltzes and foxtrots.'

'Everything is difficult for her,' Rachel said. 'And it's a terrible shame — at her age.'

Deborah came in with a tray of coffee.

'That is nice of you, dear. To make it for all of us,' Rachel spoke as to a very young child. 'I think I'll take mine upstairs, if Mr. Nicholson will excuse me. Time I was in bed. Goodnight.'

The three who were left echoed her 'goodnight'. Elaine sat on the edge of her chair, wondering if she, too, ought to go and leave the girl and the man to get to know one another. But it seemed wrong. He was much too old for Deborah. He must be near in age to herself. Or even older.

Deborah was more lively and gay than Elaine had seen her for a very long time. Usually the girl was sharp and sulky, and found it impossible to talk naturally to her mother. Now, she was like any other girl of her age, eager, excited by her outing. She flirted with Andrew Nicholson, who seemed to be intrigued by her.

When he got up to go, Deborah went to him and caught at his arm. 'When shall I . . . shall we see you again, Andrew? I've enjoyed being with you.'

He glanced at Elaine before he replied. 'Yes, why not? What about an outing? If this decent weather holds until the weekend, we could go to the coast. It would do us all good to get a breath of sea air.'

'All?' Deborah queried.

He nodded. 'We couldn't leave your mother and your gran at home, when we have spare seats in the car. Perhaps they would enjoy it.'

Deborah shrugged. 'Would you want to come, mother?' she asked.

'Yes,' Elaine replied. 'It would be better for us all to go.'

Andrew gave her a grin, before he went out with Deborah.

The girl soon came back, her cheeks

glowing. Silently, she gathered up her outdoor things, preparing to go upstairs.

'Just a moment,' Elaine said. 'I assume that you enjoyed this evening.'

'Yes, I did. Just for once. I didn't feel left out.'

'That's good. Though Mr. Nicholson said there was no reason why you shouldn't have joined in with the sort of dancing the others were doing. Except he felt you were too young for it.'

Deborah gave a little laugh. 'Did he say that? It was for your benefit. He knows that girls of sixteen aren't too young for anything these days. That is, normal girls.'

Elaine flinched. 'Is he married?' she asked.

'Not according to Pamela. You can be sure I soon found that out. Even I'm not reduced to hole and corner affairs yet.'

'I should hope not. He seems a bit old, that's all. I shouldn't have thought you would have had a lot in common.'

'Wouldn't you? You'd be surprised.

7

And he didn't go off and leave me so that he could dance with other girls, like the young ones do. He stayed with me and talked and made me laugh. With him, it seemed that I was still one of the party. I don't care how old he is. I like him.'

'Yes. I can see that you do,' Elaine said. 'At least, he's kind and thoughtful. And we'll get to know him better when we go out with him on Sunday.'

'He only asked you because he thought you wouldn't let me go alone.'

'He was quite right.'

'Goodnight.' Deborah's voice was cool as she went out, and up the stairs.

Elaine tidied the room, straightened the cushions and put away her knitting. Then she stood for a moment reflecting. He must be a kind man, this Andrew Nicholson. But she wished she knew a little more about him. This friendship was springing up too quickly. And Deborah was already getting silly ideas.

Elaine sighed. Another problem.

Another burden for her to take on herself. It was hard enough to cope with Deborah as it was. Not only was the usual adolescent rebellion spiking the girl's temper, there was also her resentment, which seemed to grow with the months and years. And if she fancied herself with a broken heart as well . . .

Elaine switched off the lights and went slowly up to her room.

The next day, Elaine realised that she'd been too precipitate in accepting the invitation to spend a day with a man they didn't know. Even if there were to be four of them. She decided to make a few discreet enquiries.

She rang Pamela Grey's mother. 'Oh, Mrs. Grey, a gentleman, named Andrew Nicholson brought Deborah home last night from your party. I felt I ought to thank him. Do you know where he lives?'

'Andrew? Yes. He's really a friend of my husband's. They meet at business occasionally. He lives in digs at 45,

Ferrybarn Street.'

'I thought he was a little old to be a friend of Pamela's.'

'He's the friend of all of us really. Dear old Andrew. We can always call on him to make up a party. So useful to know an unattached man, isn't it?'

'Yes — yes, I suppose it is. Well, thank you, Mrs. Grey. Goodbye.'

The short conversation settled Andrew Nicholson more comfortably in Elaine's mind. He was obviously the eternal bachelor, the kindly uncle, the harmless friend of both sexes. Yet, to look at him . . . Probably a day in his company would be pleasant and undemanding. So long as Deborah could get the man in perspective. Though, no doubt, by now he knew how to deal with teenage crushes.

Elaine decided to get her hair set on Saturday morning, and she bought herself a pale blue sweater to wear. Then she felt foolish when she found Deborah giving herself a face-pack, and painting her nails, fingers and toes. So Elaine gave the sweater to Deborah, and decided to wear her thick navy woolly over her white slacks.

Andrew had arranged to call for them early on Sunday morning. Rachel grumbled a little at having to get up so soon, but she didn't want to miss the outing. She thought the young man 'charming', especially to include herself and Elaine in the invitations. 'Shows he has a nice nature,' she said.

She was ready, dressed in a warm coat and with a headscarf round her hair, before it was time for Andrew to arrive.

He was prompt, and got them settled in his rather small, two-door car. Deborah stood aside to let her mother and grandmother climb into the back seats. She took the front passenger seat as by right.

They were all quiet at first, as Andrew drove through the hushed streets and joined the stream of traffic on the main road, heading for the coast.

'How far is it?' Deborah asked.

'Fifty-five miles. This is the furthest I

have ever lived from the sea. I was born in Devonshire, and we lived in Brixham until I was fourteen. So I spent my boyhood in small boats. I have to get to the sea as often as I can.'

'Do you sail?' Deborah asked eagerly.

'Not on this coast,' he answered. 'When I am able to go down south, I often do. Though I was referring to small rowing boats in my childhood.' Then he threw a few words over his shoulder, as if he had suddenly remembered his passengers in the back.

'It looks like keeping fine for us, ladies. I assume you like picnics.'

'You must have noticed that I have brought one,' Elaine answered him. 'It would be a shame to spend part of a bright day queuing at a cafe for a meal.'

'I hope you haven't brought door-step sandwiches,' Deborah put in.

'I've brought crusty rolls, butter and cheese. Will that suit you?'

'Schoolgirl appetite,' Andrew teased the girl.

'I'm not a schoolgirl,' Deborah

answered him firmly. 'I'm taking a secretarial course. I shall be qualified in a few months' time. Can you offer me a job?'

'You wouldn't like it where I work,' he said. 'It's a very dull routine. You'd need something more exciting, I'm sure.'

'Not if you were there,' Deborah said pertly. She glanced over her shoulder to see how her mother had taken this remark. But Elaine was looking out of the window. Rachel smiled at her granddaughter. For her, her dead son's child could say or do no wrong. As she so often declared, there was only Deborah to make her life worthwhile.

Andrew turned off the main road before it reached the popular resort of Stretton-on-Sea, and drove to a small village called Sandy Bay. The village must have been given its name many years ago, for now the beach was stony and deserted. The sand was concentrated in the sandhills, that sheltered the beach from the landward winds.

They took the picnic basket from the car, with a cushion or two for Rachel, and found themselves a sheltered cut-out near the bottom of a sandhill. Deborah soon had her shoes off, and she dragged Andrew to the water's edge, where she paddled and kicked, whilst he stood and watched her.

'I've never known Deborah get so fond of anyone before, have you?' Rachel asked.

'She's at the age, isn't she?' Elaine replied. 'We all get struck on older men when we are so young ourselves. Especially if they happen to be presentable and unattached.'

'She'll need someone to look after her,' Rachel said. 'A young boy would be no good for her. Make her feel her handicap too much.'

'Not if he were . . . ' Elaine stopped. It was useless to discuss Deborah with Rachel. There was too much prejudice, for the girl, against the mother. And Rachel was only too pleased to let her bitterness escape in sly remarks, that stung Elaine into remembrance of her guilt. As if she could forget it. Rachel would take good care that she never did.

Elaine got up. 'I think I'll stretch my legs for a time. Will you be all right?'

'Yes. So long as Andrew and Deborah don't go far away.'

'They're not likely to. They seem to be enjoying themselves too much. At least, Deborah does.'

She went before Rachel could observe that there were few times when the child could be really happy.

Elaine walked further than she intended. The beach was firm near to the sea. There was a breeze, and she felt a surge of energy as she breathed in the salty air.

It was not until the beach huts of Stretton came into sight that she realised that she had covered two miles. She turned to walk back. The others might wonder where she was.

She had walked towards Sandy Bay for a while when she saw a figure

15

approaching. It was Andrew. He stopped and waited for her to reach him. 'We were wanting food,' he said. 'You'd been gone for a long time. I decided I'd better come and look for you.'

'I'm sorry. I was so enjoying the air. I always feel well on this coast.'

'You look well, too, with colour in your cheeks. You were striding out like an athlete. I'm glad this outing is giving you pleasure.'

'A lot, Mr. Nicholson. We don't have the opportunity to do such trips very often.' She was conscious that this conversation was clipped and formal. So, apparently, was he.

'Can't you use my Christian name? And I'd like to use yours. It has a soothing sound. Elaine. Elaine.' He pronounced the name several times, in an almost caressing tone.

She laughed. 'I've always hated it. So old-fashioned.'

'A classical name,' he said.

She noticed that his steps were slowing, so she had to slow down too.

Then she was startled by his question. 'What happened to Deborah? What caused the limp? She makes too much of it, doesn't she?'

'It's difficult to know,' she answered in a low voice. 'She says it stops her dancing and playing games like others of her age. And it makes her feel conspicuous. I've tried to persuade her to wear built-up shoes, but she says they are heavy and uncomfortable and ugly. That's important when one is young — when one feels deprived.'

'How did it happen?' he asked again.

'In a car crash. She came out of it better than we had feared. The leg was badly hurt.'

Andrew was quiet for a few moments, but glanced at her face several times. 'It's tough on your own, isn't it? I mean, without a husband to help you.'

Elaine's voice became cold. 'I have Deborah and my mother-in-law. I'm not lonely.'

'Aren't you? I am. Most people are, if they tell the truth.'

17

'I understand that you're not married.' Elaine said.

'Not now. I'm a divorced man. So probably I'm not a suitable companion for your daughter, or for you.'

'I'm sorry,' she murmured.

'I got over it. I don't talk about it, because people think there's something wrong with you if you come out of one marriage and don't immediately rush into another.'

'Then why mention it to me?'

'Because you seem so doubtful about me — as a friend.'

'Well . . . ' she paused, embarrassed. 'Isn't it a little too soon to be talking about friendship? It takes time to get to know people.'

'Yes, usually,' he said. 'Although I . . . ' he stopped. 'Forgive me if I am too inquisitive. Do you have to live with your mother-in-law? It doesn't seem to make you very happy.'

'Happy?' she echoed, as though it were a word that didn't come into her vocabulary. 'Yes, you are inquisitive. We live with Mrs. Barrington because she has a large house, so we may as well share it as have the expense of two homes. And she likes to have Deborah near her.'

'The daughter of her dead son.'

'Yes. It's only natural.'

They were silent for a few moments. His steps were slower than ever.

'We ought to hurry,' she said. 'The others will be tired of waiting.'

'Just tell me one more thing. You may as well. How did you lose your husband?'

Elaine frowned and took a moment to reply. 'He died after the car crash that crippled Deborah.'

'Oh, I see. A double tragedy. No wonder you seem so sad. Was he driving?'

Elaine's face was contorted before she could get out the words. 'No. I was.'

She heard him draw in his breath. 'Now are you satisfied?' she demanded.

He put out a hand towards her, but she rushed ahead, wishing she could go

home. But she had to get through the
rest of the day.

Deborah and Rachel didn't notice
how quiet Elaine was that afternoon. In
any case, she was always quiet. But
Elaine felt Andrew's eyes on her many
times.

Silently she cried out to him. 'Leave
me alone, can't you? What has it to do
with you. Leave me alone. I've got to
live with it. I. I. No one else.'

2

Elaine was glad that life quickly resumed its monotonous rhythm for her and for Deborah and Rachel. Nothing was heard from Andrew Nicholson, and no one seemed anxious to mention his name.

Even the talkative Rachel referred only fleetingly to the day by the sea. 'I wish we could get out more often. It gives Deborah such a nice break. They work her too hard at the college.'

Deborah found her work difficult, and was often poring over shorthand outlines. One evening she tried to take down notes from a speaker on the radio, but gave it up after only a few lines.

'Let me help you,' Elaine offered.

'No. I have to do it for myself, haven't I? Besides, your ideas are probably out of date.'

'They still work,' Elaine replied, but got no further.

'Staying in again all evening?' Rachel asked tactlessly.

'Well, how can I go anywhere?' Deborah demanded. 'The gang from college are always either at the skating rink or dancing. So where would I be?'

'Doesn't anyone ever see a film or go to the theatre?' Rachel persisted. 'You'd enjoy that.'

'Not in a gang. You only need two for that sort of thing.' Deborah sank into sulky silence, and Rachel was quietened.

When Elaine had heated their evening drinks, she decided to go to bed. She needed plenty of rest to create the energy needed to take her through her busy days.

She was the sole office worker in the one-man firm that employed her. Then there was the housework to do and the shopping, and the cooking that was too much for Mrs. Barrington. Sometimes she felt that life demanded more than she could give.

As Elaine went upstairs, she heard Rachel switch on the television set and there was a movement in the hall. She took no notice until a few moments later, as she crossed the landing to go to the bathroom, she realised that Deborah was speaking on the telephone.

She stopped to listen. She felt guilty, but as the girl so rarely told her mother anything, Elaine had to find out in any way she could, the sort of people her daughter associated with.

She had to strain to catch Deborah's words, and she hoped the girl wouldn't look up and see her.

'Oh, there you are, Andrew. It's Deborah here. I wondered how you were getting on. It seems ages since we saw you. What — a fortnight? Seems longer than that. I thought perhaps you didn't like us after all.' She laughed at the reply.

Elaine didn't know whether she was relieved or sorry that Deborah was contacting Andrew Nicholson. The conversation went on.

'You can't be as busy as all that. I see there's a film on in town that you said you wanted to see. Oh, have you been already? I just thought ... yes, I suppose so. Won't I be seeing you at all then? Of course I have lots of work to do, but all work and no play ... Oh, Andrew.' Her voice became plaintive. 'Will you come round for coffee then? Oh, good. When? We'll be ever so glad to see you. Do you mean it?'

At this point, Elaine moved to the bathroom. She hoped Deborah wasn't making a nuisance of herself. At least Andrew had the sense to refuse to see the girl alone. Very wise of him. Elaine couldn't interfere. Not at this stage.

In the morning she waited for Deborah to mention that Andrew would be visiting the house. But the girl said no word. She went off to college looking a little more cheerful than normally.

Elaine reached her office first, as usual. Her employer Stan Davies, was a seasoned drinker, but he'd never been able to find a formula to cope with the 'morning after' queasiness.

She started to open the letters. Stan Davis described himself as a 'merchant' but he was really an agent. Goods were stocked in the old, echoing warehouse, for a number of manufacturers. A man and a boy were employed to handle the goods as they were ordered. All invoicing, correspondence and record-keeping fell to Elaine.

By the time Stan Davis arrived, his letters were in one neat pile on his desk, and his bills in another. He nodded to Elaine as he moved through her small office to his own. He was soon letting out a bellow of rage.

Elaine went next door to see if her employer had been consulting his bank statement and found himself insolvent. Instead, he was holding a tax demand in his hand. 'Have you seen this? It's an outrage. It's more than all the profit I made last year. What the hell do they think they are up to?'

'Trying to make you send proper

accounts,' she told him. 'I've done my best to persuade you to employ an accountant. He would save you much more than the fee he would charge. You're being very short-sighted about this.'

Stan glared at her. 'Well, something's got to be done. Get me an accountant, then. As soon as possible. Right away.'

Elaine smiled as she went back to her own office. She looked in the telephone directory. She knew of only one firm of chartered accountants, called, she thought, something like Simpkin and Brown.

She found the name after some searching, and rang to ask for someone to come and see Mr. Davis. She was put through to 'one of the partners', and wondered what was familiar about the voice. 'I'll be along tomorrow morning. That's the earliest I can promise,' the voice told her. And Stan had to be content with that.

Promptly at eleven o'clock the next morning, Andrew Nicholson made

Elaine's small office seem overcrowded. He was grinning at her. 'I'm the accountant you put out an s.o.s. for. Didn't you know that was my job?'

'No.' She was too surprised to say anything else.

'I recognised your voice at once. Are you sure you didn't know it was me?'

'Quite sure. I just thought there was something faintly familiar . . . '

Stan's office door opened. 'Come in here, young man. You've got to get me out of this mess. I don't know what the Inland Revenue's playing at.'

Andrew nodded to Elaine and disappeared.

The two men were together for nearly two hours. At times there were raised voices, but always it seemed that Andrew was the one to quell the other. Stan Davies had met his match.

It was nearly one o'clock when Andrew emerged. 'Whew,' he said, not caring whether Stan heard him or not. 'That's a hard nut to crack. But I think we'll get him to toe the line in time. I'm dying of hunger. Come and have lunch with me.'

'Oh, no, thank you. I've brought sandwiches for myself.'

'And you'll stay here and eat them?'

'I usually do. Then go out if I have any shopping that is urgent.'

'You need to get out. You'll suffocate if you stay in this place for a whole day. I don't like eating alone. Come on; throw the sandwiches to the birds, and keep me company at that new restaurant in the Market Place.'

Elaine started to refuse again, but Andrew reached her coat from its peg on the door, and held it for her to get into.

'Oh, all right,' she said ungraciously. 'But excuse me whilst I do something to my face.'

She was back in a few minutes. Andrew was still in her office. Stan had left for his own lunch.

'That boss of yours has been warning me off you,' Andrew said.

'Warning you off . . . what do you mean?'

'You're the best girl he's ever had. He doesn't want you upset by men chasing you.'

'Oh, really.' Elaine laughed, and suddenly felt younger and light-hearted.

Andrew had his car outside, but they decided to walk to the market place. He held her elbow to help her across busy roads, and now and then they stopped to admire something in a shop window. Andrew was in a cheerful mood, and kept away from personal topics.

They went into the newly opened restaurant and took a table by the window. Elaine was able to watch the passers-by until they were served, then turned her attention to the menu the waiter handed to her.

She swallowed when she saw the prices. 'Oh, Andrew. This is such an expensive place. I can't enjoy a meal that is costing you so much.'

'Who would consider cost when chasing a woman? According to your

29

boss, I'm chasing you. Do you mind?'

She smiled at his banter. 'Well, at least it's pleasant to feel one has someone's interest. But that's as far as the joke goes. Don't worry, Andrew. I won't mistake your motives.'

'What a pity,' he countered.

'You're my daughter's friend. No doubt you're just trying to curry favour with me, so that I won't object to the friendship.'

Andrew made no answer to this, for their food had arrived. They lingered over the meal, and Elaine had a feeling of leisure such as she had not enjoyed for as long as she could remember. Let old Stan Davis be annoyed at her lateness. He wouldn't sack her. He couldn't do without her.

'I'm quite efficient at my job,' she remarked suddenly to Andrew.

His eyebrows went up.

'I'm not very good at anything else,' she went on. 'According to my mother-in-law, I'm not a good housekeeper. According to my daughter, I'm not a good mother. My husband used to say . . . Well, I'd not have much self-respect left if I couldn't do at least one job satisfactorily.'

Andrew waited for a moment before he spoke. 'People can be too demanding, you know. They set no limit to their expectations of others — expectations that nobody could live up to.'

Elaine smiled at him. 'You are a comfortable and comforting person to be with. Thank you for this lunch. I appreciate it all the more for being able so rarely to . . . ' She didn't finish her sentence.

They walked briskly back to the office, and Andrew left Elaine at the entrance without making any mention of his visit to the house, nor of his seeing her again. Though, of course, he would be coming into the office from time to time.

Elaine had to work late to make up for the prolonged lunch break, and as she clambered on to the 'bus to take her home, she wondered whether she should mention the outing with Andrew to Deborah or to her mother-in-law. When he came to see Deborah, Andrew might mention it himself. She should be open about it. Why not? It couldn't — didn't mean anything.

The cold silence that greeted her at home stilled her tongue. What was wrong now?

She ate the cold supper that was on the table in the dining room, then she joined Rachel in the sitting room. Deborah, for some reason, was spending the evening in her room.

'What's the matter?' Elaine asked Rachel. 'You seem depressed.'

'No wonder. That child is in a state. I don't know what about. But something has upset her.'

'Why? What has she said?'

'So little that I can't make head or tail of it. About it not being fair. Everything taken away from her. Old people were selfish. I don't know whether she meant me. Heaven knows,

I give her all I can. What more can I do?'

'You give her far too much. Try to take no notice of her. She talks wildly when she's upset. I'll go and see her a little later if she doesn't come down. All teenage girls have these awkward moods. And Deborah's are no doubt emphasised because she feels herself so hard done by.'

'And isn't she?' Rachel snapped.

Elaine tried to read. All the time she was listening for sounds from her daughter's room. None came, so she decided to take the girl a glass of hot milk. She set the tray with the milk and some of Deborah's favourite biscuits, took them upstairs and tapped on her daughter's bedroom door.

There was no response. For a moment, Elaine wondered if Deborah had gone out without telling them. She tried the knob and found that the door was locked.

She knocked briskly now and called. 'Deborah, open this door. I have

33

brought you a drink.' She rattled the doorknob more loudly, and knocked again.

She waited, and there was the sound of movement from inside. The key was turned in the lock. Elaine pushed the door open and went in.

Deborah was standing, lumpily, in the middle of the room. The cover of her bed was creased where she had been lying. The girl hung her head, and Elaine guessed that her daughter's eyes were red with crying.

She put the tray down on the dressing table, and sat on the edge of the bed. 'Now, Deborah, tell me what the trouble is. Why have you shut yourself away all evening? What has upset you?'

'I don't know why you bother to ask. As if you cared I'm just a clumsy cripple that nobody wants.'

'Oh, stop this self-pity,' Elaine spoke sharply. 'The thing happened, and you have to live with it — just as I do. We've had these scenes before. They get us nowhere.'

'Easy for you to talk. You're all right. You didn't even get scratched. But me — and my daddy. If only he were here now.'

Elaine got up and moved to her daughter. 'Stop it,' she said. 'You only talk like this to torment me.'

'And what about my torment?' the girl demanded. She turned now and faced her mother. 'You're not satisfied with ruining me physically, are you? You have to snatch away the first chance of happiness that I've had.'

Elaine sat down again. 'I don't know what you are talking about so melodramatically.'

'Don't you? Don't you?'

Elaine noticed that Deborah was gripping her hands tightly, as though to keep herself from hitting her mother. 'No, Deborah, I don't. Please explain. I want your happiness before everything, as you should know by now. So how I've possibly spoiled it for you, I can't imagine.'

The girl spat out her next comment.

35

'What about lunch time then? I saw you. Sitting there in that new restaurant. Smiling and talking as if — as if — and so secretly. I've not seen Andrew since that Sunday. How many times have you met him on the quiet? Where else have you been together?'

Elaine stared at Deborah. Jealousy made the girl ugly. Elaine wanted to put her arms round her daughter, to comfort her and soothe away her ridiculous fears.

She tried to speak calmly. 'I didn't see you at lunch time, Deborah. Or you could have joined us. Andrew Nicholson is taking over the accountancy for my boss, and he came to the office. As it was lunch time, he suggested that we should eat together. This was the first time I had seen him since the outing, and I probably won't see him again.'

The mother's calmness seemed to placate Deborah a little. She spoke less shrilly. 'He's my friend. It was I who brought him here. I know he's older than me, though he's not as old as you

36

are. Anybody can see that. And if you try to take him away from me, I'll . . . '

'Stop talking so foolishly. You are being ridiculous. Now drink your milk and go to bed. I think it would be a good thing if we both dropped this man who is causing so much trouble. I may have to see him on business, but beyond that . . . '

'I'll *not* drop him,' Deborah said defiantly. 'I like him. I think of him all the time. I love him. And he likes me. I know he does. So, unless you put your spoke in . . . '

'Oh, Deborah,' Elaine sighed. 'You'll love lots of people before you find the real, lasting feeling, that can see two people through a lifetime together.'

'Is that what you and my father had? A real, lasting feeling? From what I remember . . . '

'Please, Deborah. Leave me out of this. I'm trying to help you. You are at a difficult stage of life. Young people suffer more than many grown-ups realise, but don't let yourself be torn asunder by your feelings. They'll change quickly, even from day to day. So, if only you can remember that there is always another day, another man, you won't get into such despair.'

'The way you preach at me.' Deborah had disgust in her voice. 'If you'd arranged your own life more success- fully, you might be worth listening to. But, really, mother, there's no advice that you can give me.'

Wearily, Elaine got up and went to the door. She was too tired to argue any more. And it was useless, anyway. Deborah despised the mother whom she blamed for her father's death and for her own lameness. Elaine supposed it was a natural attitude. The girl had been badly hurt. Perhaps, some day, when she was secure in her own love and happiness, she would try to understand, and to love her mother again.

Rachel Barrington was waiting for Elaine on the landing. 'I couldn't help overhearing. Is it true?'

'Is what true?'

'That you're going around with Andrew Nicholson?'

'Oh, not again,' Elaine sighed. 'Must I convince you now? That it is nothing. He came to my office and we had lunch together. Is that 'going around' with a person? I'm sorry. I'm sorry I went. I'm sorry I ever saw the man.'

'Well, he is Deborah's friend. Apart from that, even if you meet someone you like, can you forget Michael so easily? Can you forget my son. I can't. I think of him every day and the waste of his dying. And the pain that poor girl has to suffer for the rest of her life through one moment's carelessness. Can you forget all that, Elaine? And me. Alone now with no one to turn to?'

Elaine made no answer. She went into her room and shut the door, wishing she could lock it against the pair of them. Wishing she could lock out the past and the present and go to sleep. Go to sleep for ever.

3

Elaine worked steadily through the next morning, unable to control a slight lurch of the heart each time the outer door opened.

But Andrew didn't call that day. He telephoned and she put him straight through to Stan Davis, before there could be any conversation. The next morning he came with a number of queries for Stan, and Stan had just gone out for his morning drink. So Andrew waited in Elaine's office.

'Lunch again today?' he suggested.

'Sorry. I can't manage it.'

'Why not? You have to eat. And the middle of the day seems to be the only part you can call your own.'

'Not even that. I have a great deal of shopping to do, and I have to meet Deborah and go with her to the dentist.' She made that up as she spoke.

40

'Oh, well, some other time,' Andrew said. 'By the way, I'll be dropping in one evening for coffee. Your daughter invited me.'

'I heard her,' Elaine answered. 'I'd be grateful if you would stay away.'

'Oh.' Andrew was taken aback for a moment. 'Do you fear for your daughter then? That crush of hers will soon die a death, especially if . . .'

'If what?'

'If she thinks I'm interested in her mother.'

Elaine stopped typing and got up. 'Please Andrew. Life at home is too complicated. I know Deborah will get over her fancy for you — but it's not just that. I have to be responsible for her and for my mother-in-law. I have no room in my life for anyone else. Oh, can't you see how impossible it is for me?'

'No, I can't,' he said stubbornly.

Elaine sat in her chair again.

'You're how old?' Andrew went on. 'Thirty-five?'

41

'Thirty-seven,' she put in.

'Exactly the same age as me. And there's a heck of a lot of life to get through yet. Your daughter will marry and leave you. Your mother-in-law must arrange her own life as any other widow has to. You can't be their sacrificial lamb for ever.'

Elaine was saved a search for a reply as Stan Davies came in, beaming from his pick-me-up. 'Now, me lad. You've got a lot of queries, you say. Better come into my office and get them over with.'

The query session went on for a long time, and Elaine was glad to be able to put on her coat and go out for her shopping before Andrew Nicholson emerged from the other office. She spent a lot longer in the shops than necessary. She wanted to be sure he would be gone before she returned.

She wandered through all the departments in the largest store in the town, and despised herself for the feelings of envy the sight of smart dresses, expensive coats and filmy wreaths of lingerie caused within her. She had no need of these things. She had no one to dress for.

When she got back to the office with her loaded shopping basket, the place was locked up.

Elaine decided to leave early that evening. She would get most of the housework done, and leave herself a little spare time at the weekend, when she could rest and read and listen to the radio.

The 'bus took her to the avenue where Rachel Barrington's house stood at the end of a cul-de-sac. Elaine staggered a little with her load, then noticed a shabby sports car parked outside the house opposite their own.

Tim. Tim Painter must have come down from University. Of course, it was near Easter, and end of term.

She must tell Deborah, for she and Tim had been playmates as children, and still got on well together.

As she rested her basket on the

pavement for a moment, Tim came out of his parents' home, saw Elaine and came swiftly across to her. 'Carry your bag, mum?'

'Thank you, Tim. It's good to see you again. Come over for supper, will you? Deborah will be so pleased that you're home.'

Tim hesitated. 'I'm not so sure. I saw her a little while ago. She was somewhat cool.'

'Oh, take no notice of that. Girls get moods, you know. Do come.'

'All right,' Tim said and bent down, his tousle of dark hair falling over his face. He tossed it back as he lifted the heavy basket and deposited it on the doorstep for Elaine. Then he was off to fuss tenderly over his wreck of a car.

There was no sign of a meal when Elaine got inside the house. Rachel was upstairs. 'She's got a headache,' Deborah said. 'I've taken her a cup of tea.'

'That was thoughtful of you. It's as well supper isn't ready. Tim is coming over to join us.'

'Oh, you've not invited him,' Deborah protested.

'Of course. I thought you'd be glad.'

'Well, I'm not. I've grown out of spotty youths.'

'I'm sure Tim isn't spotty, and he'd not appreciate being classed as a youth. He must be twenty by now. He has only another year at University.'

'He gets on my nerves,' Deborah persisted.

'He didn't the last time he was over. So why this sudden change?'

Deborah walked out without answering.

Elaine went to have a word with Rachel, then set about preparing a meal for what she hoped would be two healthy young appetites.

Supper was an uncomfortable time. Tim and Elaine tried hard to keep up the conversation. Deborah was set on having no part in it. She made no comments, and only answered questions when she was obliged to. The sulky droop of her mouth was unbecoming. Elaine felt angry with her daughter, and sorry for Tim.

He was struggling with himself. His early training in good manners stood him in good stead. Elaine tried to help him. 'What do you plan to do during the vacation, Tim? Are you staying at home?'

'For a while. I've taken up riding. I shall be looking round for a hack here. I'll get in a bit of practice.'

'Riding?' Deborah's interest was caught. She had seen girl riders on the outskirts of the town, looking smart in their outfits, looking superior from the height their horses gave them.

'Yes. Interested?'

'How could I be interested in anything like that?'

'Why not?' Tim's voice was impatient. 'You make difficulties for yourself, don't you? Instead of trying to overcome them.'

'You don't know . . . ' Deborah started, and Elaine interrupted. 'I don't see why you shouldn't try, Deborah. They can adjust stirrups, can't they, Tim?'

'Yes, of course. You have to grip with your knees. You could do that, Deborah.'

'I don't think I . . . '

'Do go with Tim and try,' Elaine urged. 'He will help you. You'd enjoy it so much. And meet new people.' She tried not to sound over-eager.

'Give it a go,' Tim backed her up. 'I'll ring up the stables and book a quiet nag for myself and a lesson for Deborah. I'll call for you, Deb. About ten in the morning. Must fly now. Have a date. Thanks for the super grub, Mrs. B. See you tomorrow.'

He went out quickly. Deborah and Elaine stared after him, then Elaine turned to her daughter. 'You'll love riding, Deborah. There's no sensation quite like it. I used to ride a bit before I was married.'

'What can I wear?'

'Slacks will do for your first lesson. Wear them with your brown boots. If you like it, and get on well, we can think about a proper outfit. Jodhpurs and a hard hat.'

'Hmm. I'll see how I feel.' Deborah was determined not to show enthusiasm.

She went off upstairs with a vision of herself tantalising her imagination. She really should have an outfit. She hated making-do. She wanted everything to be right from the start. There might be time before ten o'clock in the morning to get a pair of jodhpurs. She'd want a black coat as well. And the hat and the switch. She doubted whether her mother would have enough money in the house — but Gran would. Gran wouldn't begrudge her anything. Gran would want Deborah to look as smart as possible. She went along to her grandmother's bedroom, ostensibly to enquire about the headache.

'It's so nice of you to come, Deborah. I feel better for seeing you.'

'Do you think you'll have to stay in bed tomorrow, Gran?'

'Oh no. I'll be up as usual in the morning. What's that? Horseriding? Oh, lovie, do you think it will be safe?'

'I can try, can't I? That is if I can get the proper things.'

'Of course you must have the proper things. I tell you what, we'll both get up early. We can be at the shops by the time they open. Then you'll be happy, won't you?'

'Thank's ever so, Gran. You really are good to me.'

'And why not? You're all I've got.'

★ ★ ★

Rachel and Deborah were on the shop doorstep before it opened the next morning. A girl came and let them in, and did her best to serve them. 'The manageress hasn't arrived yet,' she said. 'If you'd like to wait and see her . . . '

'No, I want these things at once,' Deborah said. 'Surely you can look them out for me.'

The girl set about an obviously unfamiliar task. Deborah tried on several pairs of jodphurs, and decided

49

on a light, almost cream-coloured pair. Then she went through all the jackets the girl could find. She tossed them off one by one, then went back to the first she had tried. It made her waist look slim.

The hat didn't take so long. All hats were the same, except for the sizes. Then there was the switch to choose. Rachel stood by, making no comment, merely holding her handbag at the ready. 'We'll have to be quick,' she ventured at last.

Deborah decided to change at the shop, and went off with her slacks and jumper in a parcel.

As she and Rachel walked along the avenue, Tim started to cross to call for Deborah. He stopped and stared. 'Good lord,' he said. 'That was quick work. Aren't you a bit previous with the outfit?'

'I like to do things properly,' Deborah told him. 'You'll have to wait a moment or two. We haven't had any breakfast yet, have we, gran?'

Rachel had already opened the front door, and Deborah heard Elaine's voice.

'Oh, there you are. I've been worried to death. I wondered where you had both got to. Oh, really, Deborah was it necessary to get all those things so quickly? I suppose you've paid for them, Gran.'

'If it gives me pleasure . . . ' Rachel said sharply, and went towards the dining room.

'Just make me a bacon sandwich,' Deborah told Elaine. 'Can't stop for more. Tim's champing at the bit.'

'Using the lingo already,' Tim grinned as he came in behind Deborah. 'I really can't wait, you'll have to eat the sandwich as we go along.' He went out and revved up his low-slung car. Deborah snatched the sandwich and limped after him.

The car made more noise than speed.

'Won't it go any faster?' Deborah demanded when they had left the worst of the traffic behind. Tim grunted.

51

'It's supposed to be a sports car, isn't it?' Deborah persisted. She watched Tim's face flush, and smiled to herself.

She was conscious of his pressing harder on the accelerator, but it made little difference to the labouring engine. Silly thing, Tim, trying to pretend it was a roadster when it was only a broken down old banger.

They soon reached the riding school which seemed to consist of a row of stables and several well-fenced fields. There was a house near the lane, by which they entered, and Tim called there to tell the school owner that they had arrived.

He came back with a young girl dressed in khaki breeches, with a scarf round her head. She was tanned, and Deborah noticed that her hands were slim and strong.

'This is your teacher,' Tim said. 'Miss Darwin.'

'Call me Carol.' The girl was eyeing Deborah's outfit. 'You're got up regardless, aren't you?'

Deborah's mouth tightened. If this Carol were going to be sarcastic . . . 'I have a limp,' Deborah said with defiance in her voice.

'So long as you can grip with your knees.' Carol dismissed this complication. 'Come along. The others are waiting.'

'Others?' Deborah asked, and got no answer.

Tim parked his car near the end of the lane. They walked to a field where a group of youngsters, in motley outfits, awaited them.

Tim went to the stables to get his mount, then joined a group going for a ride round the countryside. Carol fetched a couple of ponies, and stable boys followed with others.

Soon the learners were all mounted, and Carol took them in turn, on a leading rein, round the field, Deborah went first, and felt all eyes on her. She held herself proudly, and felt at home on this good-natured horse.

But it was too slow on the leading

53

rein. She wanted to go faster and faster, to feel the horse trotting and galloping. But she had no chance to try and make the creature move faster. When she wasn't on the rein, the horse's head was held by a boy.

The hour was soon over, and another group of youngsters had gathered for the next session. Deborah felt elated by her solemn ride round the field. If only she could have the horse to herself, she'd soon be riding properly. She loved the feeling of power over a big animal, and she longed for a real chance to make it obey her, respond to her demands.

Oh yes, this riding was good sport. Apart from having to adjust the stirrup, Carol had made no concessions to one pupil's lameness.

Deborah had come to the gate of the field and found a young man, leaning on his elbows, watching her. She flushed slightly under his gaze.

'My, you're a sight for sore eyes,' he said He had a cultured accent, and was expensively dressed in sports coat and slacks. 'Quite the little rider, too. You'll do well on the gee-gees. I can see that.'

Deborah regarded him. 'It was my first attempt. I felt all right. I think I shall learn quickly.'

'Good. I like confidence in a dame. Would you like a lift back to town?'

She hesitated, and looked down the lane to where the cars were parked. Next to Tim's brightly-coloured wreck was a gleaming, new sports car, with its hood down. Its lines were exaggerately graceful. Even the tyres seemed larger and heavier than was normal.

Then Deborah looked at her outfit. The almost white jodhpurs were soiled — that horse must have been dirty but she knew she still looked smart. Too good for that boneshaker of Tim's. He wasn't back yet from his ride, so why not get a lift in this smashing new car. It would be a thrill just to sit in it.

'All right, thank you.' She told the young man where she lived.

'We might have a spot of lunch

together,' he suggested. 'Unless you're in too much of a hurry.'

'Well . . . ' Deborah thought of the rest of the day stretching empty before her. 'No, I could manage that. I'd have to ring home, of course.'

'Of course. My name's Garry Leyland.' He said.

'Deborah Barrington.' She was delighted when he suggested the new restaurant in the Market Place. She felt she would be getting back at her mother by going there with Garry.

She rang her home from the restaurant. 'I shan't be in to lunch,' she told Elaine. 'I'm having it in town with a friend.'

'What friend?' Elaine wanted to know. 'Where's Tim?'

'No one you know,' Deborah answered pertly. 'I missed Tim somehow. See you soon.' She rang off on her mother's protests.

They chose a table by the window, where Deborah hoped she would be seen. Garry ordered wine with their meal. This was the first time Deborah had drunk wine in any quantity. Her previous experience had been limited to one sherry glass at Christmas and sometimes at birthdays. Today she drank freely, and Garry kept refilling her glass. This was living.

They lingered over the meal, and when, at last, Garry suggested they should go, Deborah stood up and found that the room was swimming around her. 'I think I'm a little tipsy,' she laughed.

Garry took her arm and led her out. The fresh air didn't help matters. Her head was spinning, and she scarcely knew how Garry got her to his car, but she found herself sitting in it. 'Where are we going?' she asked muzzily.

'To my flat of course. Can't send you home in this state.'

'I need some black coffee,' she said. 'Then I shall be fine.'

Gary laughed. 'We'll see. Probably hair of the dog would be better.'

Deborah's head lolled as Garry drove

swiftly from the centre of the town. She didn't notice the direction they took. Eventually, she opened her eyes and found that they had parked outside a big house, almost a mansion. 'Is this where you live?' she asked.

'In a bit of it. I have a flat here.'

He helped her out of the car, through the imposing front door of the house, up a flight of stairs and into his flat, which she realised, vaguely, was expensively and comfortably furnished.

She sank into a thickly upholstered settee, and let herself relax. Soon she felt her hard hat being lifted off her head. 'That's better,' she said.

'May as well be completely comfortable.' Garry's voice was soft. 'Come along. Let's get this tight coat off you.' She made no protest as he pulled her forward and eased her arms out of her riding jacket.

Then his arms were round her, and his mouth pressing on hers. She pushed at him futilely. She managed to drag her face round from his mouth. 'Leave me alone,' she said.

'Don't be a fool,' he retorted. 'What do you think you're here for?'

She tried to sit up, but he held her down. She felt his fingers fumbling with the buttons of her blouse. She gathered her strength together, and struck out at his face. She caught him at the side of his ear.

He recoiled. 'You vixen. You'll pay for that. What do you take me for?'

Deborah was thoroughly frightened, but suddenly he let her go. 'Look, don't let's fight. This is silly. Obviously you've not got over the lunch yet. I'll give you a pick-me-up, then you'll feel different.'

He went to a drinks trolley and started to pour a mixture of drinks into a glass. He came back and held out the glass to Deborah. She took it and sniffed at the contents. 'What is it? It might make me worse.'

'Drink it up, and see if it will put a bit of life into you.'

She took a few sips and stopped. She

stared at Garry Leyland. He wasn't good-looking any more. His face was flushed and his eyes protruded. His mouth was slightly open.

Deborah was trying to make her fuddled brain function. She had to outwit this man. He was a challenge and she would get the better of him. She was still afraid, but enjoying her fear. This was life — living.

She tossed back the rest of the contents of the glass, and sat up. 'I'm not the fool you take me for,' she told the man. 'So you can stop your little tricks. I wasn't born yesterday.'

He laughed. 'Where did you hear that? In a film?'

Deborah got unsteadily to her feet. Her head seemed to be clear now, and a great stimulation was surging through her veins. She felt she could fight Garry and more like him.

He put down his own glass, taking her move as an invitation. Then he held her against him with one arm, his other exploring her body.

She struggled, brought up her fists and pummelled him, but this did not stop him. He held her closer, trapping her fists, pressing his mouth again on hers.

She felt herself being borne backwards on to the settee once more. She kicked out, and he swore, his grip becoming cruel. Then he started to tear at her clothes.

She shouted in terror now. 'Leave me alone, you great brute. You know I'm a cripple. Coward. Coward.'

'Shut up, you stupid fool,' he said between his teeth. He was hurting her badly now. She squirmed and cried and hit out when she could.

He brought up a hand and swung his palm at her face. The sting on her cheek silenced her for a moment. Then she began to struggle again, desperately this time, for she knew she was being beaten. He was on top of her, pressing the breath out of her body, swearing softly into her ear.

She turned her head and spit in his

face. This enraged him, and he rained blows on her face and head. She tried to retaliate, but was helpless under his weight. They were both grunting for breath when the doorbell shrilled and stilled them.

Deborah recovered first and heaved the man away from her. He rolled on to the floor. He got up, pulling his clothes to rights. 'Get out of here,' he said in a low voice. 'My visitor mustn't see you.'

Deborah was sober now, trying to hold her torn blouse together for some sort of cover. 'I'll stay and tell them what you tried to do to me.'

He gave her a slap over the mouth. 'One word from you, and I'll say it was your own fault. You made the running. Come on, get into that room down there, and keep quiet.'

He grabbed up her jacket and hat and pushed her with them into a small, dark room at the end of a short passage. The doorbell was screaming out again. He locked the door hurriedly, and was off.

Deborah strained to hear voices. Garry must have closed the lounge door, for she could only catch the sound of laughter now and again. Some of the laughter was feminine.

She pulled on her jacket and hat, and pondered on the advisability of banging on the door to attract attention. But that might get her into worse trouble, if Garry's friends were anything like him. She looked round to see if there was any way of escape.

The window overlooked the roof of a bay window below. Deborah didn't think the bay looked too far from the ground. She had a struggle to release the catch on the old-fashioned sash window. She broke it with the heel of her boot. Then, with the window open wide and the boot back in place, she climbed over the sill and let herself gently on to the sloping roof of the downstairs window.

Once there, she slid, unable to find anything to cling to. The drop to the ground was bigger than she had anticipated and she took it more quickly than she had planned. She lay, bruised and breathless, on the gravel of the drive. Her hat saved her from any damage to her head.

She waited for someone to come and see what the noise was all about, but no one did. So she struggled to her feet and limped towards the road. She had no idea where she was. This part of the town was quite new to her. She walked along, trying to guess the direction of the town centre, and she decided to thumb a lift. But when a car slowed up and she saw the man at the wheel, she turned quickly into a side street. She didn't want a repeat of her recent experience.

Shops appeared at more regular intervals now so she guessed she was on the right road. Between some buildings on the right, she caught sight of cranes, warehouses and the masts of boats. She was near the river, but on the wrong side of it.

She went down a street, climbed over

a wall, and walked along the embankment, which soon gave way to a towpath. She could find her way home now. She would cross the river by the bridge next to the Rowing Club. And from there, it would be easy.

She went on, her foot aching badly, her body feeling battered, her head drumming. She heard Garry's voice echoing in her head. 'You stupid fool. You stupid fool.'

Those were the words her father had used to her mother just before ... 'You stupid fool.' Well, Deborah wouldn't be stupid again. She'd learned a lot today. A lot she would never forget.

But she was so tired. She ached all over. Her head, her arms, her body. Her lame leg — that was really bad. She would have to rest for a while. The grass was thick near the river edge, and there was a group of bushes for shelter. Gingerly, she let herself down on to the ground. It was as though she were in the river itself. A heavy weight pressed itself on her head, and she closed her eyes on the pain. Then the drink took its full effect, and she fell asleep.

★ ★ ★

Rachel was crying. Elaine was pacing up and down, unable to keep still. It was one o'clock in the morning, and Deborah hadn't come home.

There was a knock on the front door. Elaine ran to open it, dreading to see a policeman there. It was Tim.

'She hasn't got back then?'

'No.' Elaine's voice sounded dead. She went back to the sitting room and the young man followed. His face was set with worry. 'Don't cry,' he said to Rachel. 'No news is good news. You would have heard if . . . if anything had happened.'

'How could you let her go away on her own?' Rachel sobbed. 'Why didn't you stop her and bring her home?'

'She went off before I got back from the ride. I told you. I never even saw

66

her after I'd left her taking a lesson. I asked everybody if they'd seen her. One girl said she'd gone off with a man in a sports car, but nobody knew who he was.'

'And she didn't tell me his name when she rang up at lunch time.' Elaine looked at Tim's distracted face. 'You mustn't blame yourself, Tim. You could have done nothing more. Deborah is so headstrong, and wherever she went, she should have been back before now. I . . . ' She stopped speaking, for she realised what she must do.

She went into the hall, picked up the telephone, dialled a number and waited, drumming her fingers, for an answer to her call. It came at last.

'I have to speak to Mr. Nicholson. Yes, I know it's late. But this is urgent. Otherwise, I wouldn't have disturbed you. Thank you. Tell him it is Mrs. Barrington.'

She waited again, then his voice came anxiously. 'Elaine. What's the matter?'

'Deborah. She hasn't come home.

Have you seen her today, Andrew?'

'No. I haven't seen her since that Sunday. How long has she been gone?'

Elaine told him what had happened. 'We don't know where she went after lunch.'

'Try not to panic. Have you notified the police?'

'No. I didn't know how long before someone became a missing person. Shall I tell them now?'

'Yes. Ring them straight away. And I'll be with you in a few minutes. Keep your courage up, my dear.'

'Andrew, I'm frightened,' she said.

'I know.'

He rang off and Elaine contacted the police, who tried to soothe her. They took down particulars, and promised to let Elaine know as soon as they found out anything about Deborah. 'There's not been an accident,' the policeman reassured her. 'Or we would have known about it. So try not to worry. We'll be in touch.'

Elaine went back to Rachel and Tim,

68

who sat silently. They had listened to her conversation so she had nothing to explain. The ticking of the clock on the mantelpiece seemed loud and mocking.

They started at the sound of a car drawing up and a quick rat-tat on the door. Elaine went to let Andrew in. He held her against him for a few moments as they stood in the hall. 'My dear,' he whispered. 'It will be all right.' She nodded and they joined the others in the sitting room.

'Isn't there anything we can do, sir?' Tim wanted to know.

Andrew grimaced at the 'sir' and glanced at Elaine. 'Yes, we can go and look for Deborah.'

'Where?' Elaine asked.

'Around the town. Anywhere. You got a conveyance, young man?'

Tim nodded.

'Take that and scour the streets between here and the outskirts of Deepway Hill. Don't miss the side streets, will you? I'll go the other way, towards the river.'

'The river,' Elaine shuddered. 'I'll go with you, Andrew.'

'But suppose the police want to get into touch with you.'

'Rachel's here,' Elaine said. She couldn't stay herself, helpless, doing nothing.

Andrew insisted on a warm coat and scarf for Elaine, and they set off at a crawl, going down all the side roads, retracing their path where there were dark shadows.

They came on a gang of youngsters weaving their way home after a dance. Andrew stopped the car and pretended to ask the way. Deborah was not with girls who crowded round, offering advice.

After that the streets were empty save for the odd cat that streaked through the headlights. Here and there upstairs rooms were lit, and Elaine envied the people who could go to bed with a quiet mind. She was sure their search would be fruitless.

The streets petered out into a field

that divided the town from the river. Andrew cut across it and started to bump slowly along the towpath. 'Oh, God,' Elaine breathed, feeling sick with every lurch of the car. The river gleamed like black silk.

Andrew stopped the car. 'What's that, I wonder.' He was looking across the river at the lights of a car on the opposite bank. 'We'll go and have a look.' He reversed the car, deeming it safer than trying to turn where the path was narrow. Elaine sat with her hands clenched, impervious now to the tossing of the car. At last it was jerked from the grass on to the road that led to the bridge.

They crossed the bridge at speed, and were soon jolting again on the river bank. 'It's a police car,' Elaine said. 'Do you think . . . ?'

'Hold on, my love,' Andrew said.

'Have they pulled . . . someone out of the river?'

'No. There'd be more activity. Don't jump to conclusions.'

Soon they were near enough to the police car to stop. Both Andrew and Elaine got out and ran to the group near to the other car. Two policemen were holding Deborah up between them.

'Is she . . . ' Elaine stopped running. At that moment Deborah broke free from the policemen's hands and went towards her mother. Elaine took her daughter in her arms. 'Are you hurt? What has happened, Deborah?' Elaine's voice was thin with anxiety.

'No, I'm not hurt. Nothing much has happened. I got lost, that's all, and I was tired. I went to sleep.'

'It must have been a deep sleep,' a policeman said. 'She took some rousing. Had a drop to drink, hadn't you, miss?'

'Only some wine at lunch time. I'm not used to it.' Deborah wasn't going to tell anyone of her humiliating experience. She had been a fool, but there was no need for everyone to know it.

'Oh, Deborah,' Elaine tried to pull

her daughter closer, but the girl stepped away, as though she couldn't bear to be touched.

'We'll take her home,' Andrew told the constable. 'Thanks for all your help. I suppose you'll report that she has been found.'

'Yes, I'll radio the station now. Glad it's nothing worse. But I should keep an eye on her. Goodnight.'

Deborah, Elaine and Andrew got into his car without speaking. He drove quickly back to the Barrington house. When he had drawn up outside the house, he turned to Deborah. 'Are you going to tell us what really happened?'

'I've already told you,' Deborah said defiantly. 'Anyone can get lost, can't they? Anyone can fall asleep.'

'What about the friend you had lunch with,' Elaine said. 'Was it a man or a girl?'

'What does it matter?'

'Of course it does,' Elaine reproached her daughter. 'Who was this person? And when did you leave him — or her?'

'Someone I met at the stables. No one you know.'

'Then your mother ought to know,' Andrew put in.

'You mind your own business,' Deborah said rudely. 'It's all your fault, anyway. I thought you were going to be my friend. I rang you, and you said you'd come. But you never did. I might have gone out with you, if you'd asked me. Then I'd have been all right, wouldn't I?'

'Aren't you all right now?' Elaine exclaimed.

'Of course I am. I said so, didn't I?'

'Then why all the secrecy?' Andrew asked.

'There isn't any secrecy. Stop going on at me. I'm all in and very cold.'

'Of course, darling. Come inside.' Elaine opened the car door. 'Gran is worried sick. We must put her mind at rest.'

Rachel embraced Deborah, who winced at the kisses. Elaine tried to look closely at her daughter, for she wasn't sure whether that was dirt or the shadow of bruises on her face. 'Are you sure you're not hurt?'

'How many more times have I to tell you,' Deborah's voice rose in irritation. 'Leave me alone, can't you? I'm back and I'm all right. So let the matter drop now.'

Elaine sighed and turned to Andrew. 'Let it go for now,' he advised. 'She'll have to tell you sometime. I expect Deborah wants to go to bed.'

'Yes,' Rachel fussed. 'Do that, love. And I'll bring you some hot milk. Are you hungry?'

'No. Cold.'

'I'll get a hot water bottle and some extra blankets. I have some of those pretty knitted ones in my blanket chest. Go along, Deborah, I'll look after you.'

Deborah went upstairs and Rachel hustled to the kitchen.

Elaine turned to Andrew. 'You don't believe it — about her being lost, do you?'

'Do you?' he parried.

She shook her head. 'I don't know

what to think. And we shan't get the truth out of Deborah if she doesn't want us to have it.'

They heard the screech of worn brakes. 'Tim,' Elaine exclaimed. She went to the front door and called to him. 'She's back, Tim. The police found her on the river bank.'

'Oh?' Tim came in, his voice full of queries.

'Come across in the morning. Perhaps she'll tell you more than she's willing to tell us. She's gone to bed now because she's cold and tired.'

'Right. I'll do that. If I'd found her, I might have told her what I think about this sort of thing. She needs a firm hand, that girl.'

Elaine's smile was reluctant. 'Thank you for trying to help, Tim.' He grunted and went to his own home.

Andrew was still in the sitting room. 'Hadn't you better go, too, Andrew?' Elaine asked him. 'It was wrong of me to drag you out, but I thought she might have gone to you.'

'I'm glad you did, Elaine. I hope you will always call on me when you are in trouble. All I want is to look after you. You know that.'

Elaine felt her colour rise. 'You are very kind . . . very . . . I'm sorry I can't . . . I'm sorry . . .'

'Don't be. I haven't really started yet, you know.'

'Started what?'

'Chasing you.' He caught her and gave her a quick kiss before he strode off and got into his car.

'Andrew,' she said, knowing he couldn't hear her.

She listened until the sound of his engine throbbed into silence, then stood for a moment, her face hidden in her hands. Then she straightened her shoulders and went upstairs, to help her daughter and her mother-in-law.

4

When Elaine took a breakfast tray to Deborah the next morning, she was horrified to see the bruises on her face. The girl was pale this morning, and the staining was coloured from brown, through purple to blue.

'However did that happen?' Elaine demanded.

'Oh, I fell and bumped myself.'

'Fell from the horse? Didn't anyone do anything about it?'

Deborah shrugged and didn't answer.

'I shall ring the riding school and complain. You must have hurt yourself very badly. Why didn't you tell me straight away?'

'Because I don't want a fuss. I don't want you to ring the riding school. It was my own fault. And it looks worse than it really is. So — for goodness sake, stop fussing.'

Deborah showed no sign of regret for the anxiety she had caused, and still she would say nothing of what happened after she had left the riding school. Elaine left her, knowing that Rachel would soon be cosseting her unrepentant grandchild.

Tim called soon after Rachel had left for church. Elaine sent him up to see Deborah, who was still in bed.

'Good lord,' he said as he came into the bedroom. 'Who's knocked you about like that? That bruise is like an ink stain. I can see it under the muck you've spread around it.'

Deborah touched her face gently. She had used a tinted face cream and suntan powder to try and hide the discoloration, but Tim had keen eyes.

'If anyone attacked you, you'd better tell me, and I'll go for him,' Tim said firmly.

Deborah looked at him calculatingly. 'Would you?'

'You know I would. Where does he live?'

She didn't answer his question. 'I did have a bit of trouble. If I tell you about it, swear you won't pass it on to mother or gran or anyone for that matter.'

'Why not? Were you to blame?'

'Maybe a bit. And they'd go on and on about it. I was able to take care of myself.' Deborah didn't say that it was only an intervention that had saved her.

'Who was the chap you left the riding school with?'

'His name's Garry Leyland. He went a bit too far, that's all.'

'All!'

'I tell you, I coped.'

'If I ever meet him. I'll go for him. I don't like chaps who treat young girls like that. Where did you say he lived?'

'I didn't. He has a flat in a big house. I'm not quite sure where it is.'

'But you went there.'

'Yes.'

'You little fool,' Tim was angry. 'Didn't you know better than that?'

Deborah closed her mouth. She had said enough.

Tim asked a few more questions, to which she gave no answers, and when his patience ran out, he went away.

He let himself out, after shouting 'good-morning' to Elaine in the kitchen, and he met Andrew Nicholson on the doorstep. Andrew took advantage of the open door to get into the house without ringing the bell.

He went straight to the kitchen, and as he had hoped, Elaine was alone. She was startled at the sight of him. He explained how he had got in. 'I wanted to talk to you on your own. How are you feeling this morning? You looked ill last night.'

'It was the worry. I'm all right now. And so is Deborah, except she has a badly bruised face. She says she fell off her horse. I've let her stay in bed for a time.'

'Fell off her horse! A likely story. But never mind that. Where's Mrs. Barrington?'

'At church. Sit down. I'll make you some coffee.'

81

Andrew sat as he was told. He watched Elaine moving about the kitchen. 'You need some fresh air,' he said. 'I know it's rather cold out, but let me take you for a run this afternoon. We could go into the country, park the car, and walk for a little while. Please say you'll come, Elaine.'

She turned to him, tempted by the invitation. Then 'No. I'm sorry. I couldn't leave them today.'

'Why not? Will they starve without you?'

She shook her head. 'They wouldn't like it.'

Andrew exploded. 'Then let them lump it. Even a slave gets time off. Don't be such a fool, Elaine. You must have some life of your own.'

She looked at him, and her lips quivered. 'Don't you understand even yet? I killed the father of one, the son of the other. I can never make it up to them, can I? But I have to do what I can. Besides, Deborah would create a scene. She regards you as her property.'

He got up, defeated. 'All right. We'll take them with us. How are we ever going to get to know one another properly, you and I? I'm attracted to you, Elaine. It may be only physical. I don't know. We need to have time together, to talk, to learn all about one another. We must, Elaine. We need one another.'

She shrugged and turned her face away. He took one of her hands, but let it go as he heard the front door open. Rachel Barrington came in. 'Oh, Mr. Nicholson. You've come to see Deborah. How kind of you. She'll be so pleased, won't she, Elaine?'

Elaine nodded and reached out another coffee cup.

'I came to see if you would all come for a car ride this afternoon,' Andrew lied. 'I think you all need a change after yesterday's upset. I'll go and see Deborah. She may not feel up to going out.'

'She will,' Rachel assured him. 'With you.'

When he had gone, Rachel turned to Elaine. 'I do hope he'll see more of Deborah now. She needs a strong, steady hand, and she likes him so much. If he had been around, yesterday wouldn't have happened.'

'Perhaps he isn't interested in anyone as young as Deborah. He's a mature man. He may prefer someone far more grown up.'

'Then he's not like most men, is he? They go for the 'dolly birds' as they call them. And even with her handicap, Deborah is a most attractive girl.'

Elaine said no more.

Deborah got up for her lunch, her face plastered with thick make-up. Andrew called for them soon afterwards.

He drove into the country, where the thin sunshine of spring was gilding the bare tree branches, urging them back to life. He parked outside a small village, and said, 'Elaine and I will take a short walk. Just over the top of that hill and back. The exercise will be good for us, and we can get some oxygen into our lungs.'

'I'll come,' Deborah said promptly. 'Mother can stay here with Gran.'

'Oh no,' Andrew answered. 'You still need to rest. You were up half the night, and in a wretched state. You mustn't exert yourself.'

'But I want to come,' Deborah insisted.

Rachel came to Andrew's rescue. 'I think Andrew is right, love. He's only thinking of what's best for you. You do need rest after your ordeal.'

Deborah slumped into her seat to sulk. Andrew nodded to Elaine, and they went off along a footpath at the edge of a field. They were careful to keep well apart whilst they were in sight of the car.

When they were over the brow of the hill, Andrew stopped and turned to Elaine. 'Now we'll have a quarter of an hour or so. There are so many things I want to ask you about. Where shall we start? With the thing that is overshadowing your life?'

'No,' Elaine said sharply.

'Tell me about the accident.' His voice was insistent.

'No. I'd rather not. Must we spoil a pleasant afternoon? I want to forget my worries. Not to talk about them. Come on, let's go a little further.'

But Andrew did not move. 'Haven't you discovered that a secret worry festers? It needs to be brought out, examined and judged. Otherwise it becomes enlarged beyond bearing. Tell me about it, Elaine. I shall have to know sometime.'

'Why? Why will you have to know?'

'So that I can completely understand you, my dear. And, I hope, help you. As I shall need your help — when you hear the worst about me.'

'No.' Elaine said again, rather violently. And Andrew was silent for some minutes.

'Come along,' she started to move. 'We must turn back. They'll be cold, sitting there in the car.'

'All right. But just tell me one thing.

Do you find me at all attractive, Elaine? Do you think you could ever . . . '

She stopped him, and she sounded irritable. 'How do I know? How can I? I'm a woman — not too old, it may be that because I've not had . . . affection . . . or anything . . . for a long time, I . . . what are you trying to make me say?'

'I just want you to agree that we need time and opportunity to find out about ourselves.'

She looked at him for a moment, then turned and walked away. She was back over the brow of the hill before he could reach her, and he hurried to catch her up. As he lengthened his stride down the field, he caught his foot in a rabbit hole, and crashed to the ground.

Elaine ran back to him. 'Are you hurt?'

'My ankle,' he said. 'It hurts like the devil.' Then he groaned.

'Oh dear, do you think you can stand on it?' Elaine asked. She tried to help him to his feet, but he sank back, his face pale and twisted with pain.

Deborah had seen his fall, and came running towards them. 'Andrew. What happened?'

'I caught my foot in a hole. I think I've sprained it.'

Elaine went on her knees and lifted his trouser leg away from his ankle, and found that his sock bulged over his shoe. That was a sprain all right.

'Look at the swelling,' said Deborah. 'You won't be able to walk or to drive.'

'We must get him to the car,' Elaine told her daughter. 'Help me, please.'

Andrew clung to Elaine and managed to stand on one leg. Deborah went to his other side and held out her arm for him to grip. He tried his injured foot on the ground, but it would not take his weight.

'You'll have to hop,' Deborah told him.

'And I'll have to lean on you both. I'm sorry, girls.' Slowly and painfully, they moved down the field.

When they reached the road, Rachel was out of the car, holding the door open for Andrew on the passenger side. 'Let me sit here for a few moments,' he said, lowering himself on to the roadside grass. 'Perhaps the pain will go off.'

'We need cold water bandages,' Elaine said practically. 'They should control the swelling. I'm sure someone in these cottages will help us.' She went to the nearest house, and soon came back with strips of bandage and a basin of cold water.

When Andrew took off his shoe and sock, Elaine was dismayed to see the deep bruise round the red swelling. She said nothing, but started to bathe the ankle, so that he shrank from the cold and the pain of it. 'Steady,' he said. 'It really does hurt.'

'We must get you a bit better,' Deborah said. 'Or how are we going to get home?'

'Yes,' Rachel echoed. 'You won't be able to drive.'

Andrew glanced at Elaine, whose pulse started to race. 'I don't suppose I shall. It's a good thing we have another driver with us.'

'No. No. I don't drive now.' The colour had left Elaine's face. 'I've not driven since . . . '

'Then it's time you started again.'

'Not with me in the car,' Deborah said. 'I don't want her to drive me ever again.'

'I should think not,' Rachel put in. 'I'd be terrified with Elaine at the wheel.'

Andrew looked round at them all. 'That's a fine attitude, I must say. Boost Elaine's confidence quite a lot.'

'If you knew what she has done to me . . . ' the girl exclaimed.

'I do know. But I still think you should trust your mother to take care of you in the car.'

'Trust her. I'd rather walk for a hundred miles than put my life in her hands again.'

'Yes,' Rachel Barrington supported

her granddaughter. 'You don't know what you're asking, Mr. Nicholson. Why, if Elaine took the wheel, it would bring it all back to Deborah — and to me. Don't forget that my son died . . .'

'You talk as if she did it on purpose,' Andrew's voice was low and angry. 'Well, you haven't much choice have you? I doubt whether there's a 'bus through this village on a Sunday. You'd better enquire at the cottages, and see if you can stay with the people until we can get back to town and send a taxi for you.'

'That will cost a lot,' Rachel quavered.

'We can't worry about that.'

Elaine stood in front of Andrew. 'Don't make me drive, Andrew. Don't make me, please.'

He reached up and took her hands. 'I want you to take me home, Elaine.'

'Can't we ring for an ambulance?'

'We could if it were serious. But I just have a sprained ankle. We have a car and we have a driver. It's only your fear that is a difficulty.'

'I can't do it, I tell you.'

'You can. You will — for me.'

Rachel walked away impatiently, and after a moment Deborah followed her.

'Now,' Andrew said. 'Give me a pull up. I'll hop to the car.'

She still hesitated. 'Please, Elaine. I'd like to get the sprain seen to.'

Elaine gripped his wrist and pulled him up. He wobbled on one leg, put an arm round her shoulders, and hopped to the car. Deborah and Rachel turned to watch them.

Elaine opened the car door on the passenger side, and Andrew lowered himself into the seat and swung his legs into the car. 'Now.'

Elaine walked slowly round the car, and stood, reluctant to get in. 'Come on, love,' Andrew urged. 'The pain's getting worse. The ankle's thumping like the devil.'

Elaine looked at him. She knew his complaining was for her sake, to try and make her forget herself, to try and make her forget her fears in a need to help him. This thought forced her stiff body into the driving seat of Andrew's car.

He started to explain the controls. They were so similar to the car she had driven before, that they did not trouble her. But her gaze still implored him. 'Don't make me,' her eyes were pleading.

He turned away from her. 'Get on with it. I won't watch you.'

Her hand trembled violently as she pulled the starting knob. And as the engine throbbed, her whole body shook. She waited for a few moments, her hands gripping the steering wheel, before, with care, she let in the clutch.

The car started to move, and Elaine was unable to keep it steady. She felt it swerve, and heard Rachel Barrington cry out. 'She's doing it again. Stop her. Stop her, Deborah.'

Through the driving mirror, Elaine saw Deborah start to run towards the car. As though to escape from her daughter, Elaine's foot pressed the accelerator and the car's pace increased. She moved the gears without having to think. She was driving again.

They went round the bend at the end of the village street, so that they were out of sight of Deborah and Rachel. 'That's better,' Andrew said. 'You'll be all right now.'

'All right on this country road,' Elaine muttered. 'We have it to ourselves.'

Andrew's voice was caressing. 'I know what this is costing you, Elaine. And I know that you're doing it for me. Thank you, my darling. You are brave, and I love you.'

Elaine couldn't answer. She was biting her bottom lip, and sat tense, holding the steering wheel far too tightly. There was a steep hill rising to the main road, and she found herself changing down at just the right moment. Experience and instinct could not be suppressed.

It was when they paused at the

junction of the country road with the main road that Elaine's heart banged the hardest. Cars were rushing along the main road, and she felt that each one was coming to crash into her. She stopped the engine. 'I can't go any further,' she said.

Andrew half turned in his seat. 'There's someone waiting behind you,' he reminded her. 'Just turn the corner so that we are out of the way.' She started the engine again, waited for two cars to pass, let in the clutch and turned the corner into the main road. There was a break in the traffic, so she went on for some yards.

'It's all clear, so you may as well keep going,' Andrew said. So she went on, flinching every time a car passed her, which they all did, as she was moving so slowly.

'Try to keep up a bit better,' Andrew advised her. 'You won't feel so much in the way.' She knew he was right. She was in the middle of the traffic now. She had to keep going.

She lifted her head, as though pride were taking over. And she drove as she had been used to driving, moderately fast, skilfully and sure. But she didn't relax until she had drawn up at the door of Andrew's lodgings. Then she sat exhausted.

Andrew put a hand over hers. 'Well done. Well done. You need never be afraid again. I'll get into the house now, then I'll ring for an ambulance. I expect I'd better have a check at the hospital.'

She turned and looked at him. 'I can take you.' She turned the car round and drove to the hospital casualty department. It was only when Andrew had hopped away to be attended to that Elaine remembered Deborah and Rachel. Hastily, she found a public telephone and ordered a taxi to fetch them. Then she sat down to wait for Andrew.

He came out hobbling with the aid of a stick. 'Only a sprain,' he said. 'They X-rayed me and bound me up. It feels much more comfortable now.'

Elaine was still weak and apt to

tremble, but she strengthened her voice and said 'I'll help you to the car and get you home.'

She was so concerned for his comfort, that she almost forgot her nervousness, and drove instinctively, as in the old days. When they were outside the house in Ferrybarn Street, she hesitated, then said, 'Will you be looked after here? Would you — would you like to stay with us until you can get around again. We could see that you rested your foot and got proper meals.'

Andrew took her hand once more. 'Darling,' he said, 'I'd like to live with you — but not with your responsibilities. I don't think I could cope with Rachel's grumblings and Deborah's demands on my attention — not at the moment. Do you mind? Do you understand?'

She nodded, annoyed at the sag of disappointment that came with his words. She got out of the car, rang the doorbell for the landlady, then helped Andrew to the door.

Mrs. Green gave an exclamation of dismay when she saw her lodger's bandaged foot. 'Dear me. Help me get him to his room,' she instructed Elaine.

Elaine helped all she could, relieved that the woman was sensibly getting Andrew comfortably settled before asking questions. She was glad, too, to find he had a pleasant room in which to live. There were shelves of books, and several reading lamps over deep arm-chairs. A record player stood near the fireplace, which held a gas fire. Elaine could picture Andrew relaxing here, listening to music and reading. But even in her pleasure, there was a hint of pain. No wonder he couldn't face the prospect of living in her own prickly household.

Her head was aching as she drove Andrew's car towards her home. She had promised to keep it in the garage until he was able to drive it again. 'Use it whilst it's there,' he had told her. 'Much better for it than standing for weeks.'

Elaine had smiled her thanks, knowing full well that she wouldn't take advantage of this invitation. She had driven today because there had been no alternative. But she couldn't face the ordeal again. It reminded her too vividly of the last time she had held the steering wheel of a car. No, she couldn't do it again.

As she turned the corner into the avenue, she saw the taxi drawing up outside Rachel's house. She drove Andrew's car into the garage at the side of the house, as the taxi waited for Rachel to fetch enough money to pay the driver.

Rachel stayed on the doorstep until the taxi had gone and Elaine joined her. 'Three pounds it cost me,' Rachel grumbled. 'And kept us waiting all that time. Most uncomfortable in that cottage. They gave us a cup of tea, but we didn't know what to talk about. I was glad to get away, so was Deborah.'

'You could have come with us,' Elaine felt and sounded sulky.

'I'd pay a lot more than three pounds to avoid that. You'd better get some hot milk for Deborah. She's ever so tired. I sent her to bed.'

Wearily, Elaine did as she was told. Her steps were slow as she went upstairs to her daughter's room. Deborah was already undressed and in bed. Her hair was spread over the pillow. 'Your grandmother's sent you this,' Elaine said.

'Ugh. I hate hot milk. Why can't I have a real drink. Whisky or something.'

'Don't be silly, Deborah.'

'Silly. That's all you ever say to me,' Deborah retorted rudely. 'I suppose I was silly to let you go off with Andrew and leave me behind. I was torn, I can tell you. I wanted to look after him, but I couldn't with you driving. Not after last time. I was terrified when I saw you driving off. If you had done to Andrew what you did to my father . . . Mother, you've got to realise this. I love him and I mean to marry him when I'm a bit older. So you can stop interfering or pretending to yourself that . . . '

'That what?' Elaine's voice was quiet and penetrating.

'That he fancies you. He only tries to please you so that you'll not be too awkward when he wants to marry me.'

Elaine sighed and turned away. She didn't want to argue with Deborah. She was too tired. And she didn't imagine that Andrew fancied her. She knew. He had told her. But how could she ever respond to his love? Deborah would take it as another way of hurting her, of impeding her happiness in life, as she so often declared the car accident had done.

Elaine went to her room and lay down on the bed, too exhausted to get undressed.

5

Elaine restrained herself from enquiring about Andrew's progress. She heard how he was getting along from Stan Davis, who was in touch with Andrew's office, and who resented having to deal with a clerk instead of with a partner.

And, of course, Deborah was not only a frequent enquirer — she rang Andrew's landlady every day — but she visited him several times each week. She borrowed money from her mother to buy tobacco, fruit and paperback books. When she wanted to buy a record, she went to Rachel for the money.

Elaine decided Andrew was having enough fuss made of him, without her adding to it.

The days dragged slowly along, and Elaine felt that she was safely back in her rut, with no Andrew to disturb her.

She was startled when Deborah reminded her that her daughter's seventeenth birthday was a mere couple of weeks away. 'I want a party, of course,' Deborah said.

'Of course,' Rachel echoed. 'Who do you want to invite?'

'I think Andrew will be able to make it,' Deborah announced gaily. 'He'll get a taxi. He said mum could fetch him in his own car, but I insisted I wanted him here in one piece.'

'Don't you want to invite anyone else?' Rachel asked.

'Not really. But as it's a party, I suppose I'll have to bring along a couple of girls from the college. Oh, and Tim said he'd come home for my birthday.'

'Oh, good,' Elaine said. 'I'm glad. I didn't know you kept in touch with him.'

'He keeps on writing. I hardly ever answer his letters.'

'Then you are rude and unkind.' The mother reproved her daughter.

'I can't be bothered with kids.' Deborah went off upstairs.

Elaine turned her thoughts to the party. She had to plan a menu and work out how and when she could make all the preparations. She wondered if, as at all Deborah's parties, she and Rachel would be expected to keep out of the way, so that young enjoyment could be unrestrained. It would seem absurd if Andrew were there. Yet Deborah would want it.

Tim came home for the weekend before Deborah's birthday. 'Are you going riding again?' Elaine asked Deborah on the Saturday morning.

'No. I don't fancy going any more. Not to that place anyway. And Tim says there's not another riding school for miles.'

'But surely,' Elaine protested, 'when your grandmother has spent so much money on your outfit. You just can't do this sort of thing, Deborah.'

'Oh, the gear will come in useful some-time,' Deborah answered carelessly. 'I didn't know I shouldn't like it, did I?'

'You should have waited to find out before causing that expense. Really, it is very selfish of you . . . '

'Oh, belt up, mother. Gran doesn't mind. So I don't see why you should. Tim's going to teach me to drive his car, so there won't be time for anything else.'

Elaine stared. 'I thought you were too nervous after — after what happened.'

'I've got to get over it. And Tim says this is the best way. And I shall make a good job of it, you'll see. No-one will be afraid to ride with me.'

Elaine coloured. 'Can you get a provisional licence?'

'Yes. I'm near enough to seventeen — only three days away. I'll be able to use Andrew's car and fetch him to the party next week.'

'You'll do no such thing. Leave that car alone. Tim said you could learn on his. So do that.'

Deborah pulled a face. 'You just never stop, do you? Do this, Don't do that. I'm not a kid any more, and I'm sick of being ordered around. There's Tim now. I'm off.'

Elaine watched through the window as the girl got into Tim's car. He had carefully tied on the L plates, and they sat as he explained the controls to Deborah. After a while, the little wreck of a car jerked and jumped along the road. Deborah had started to drive.

Elaine and Rachel saw little of Deborah for the rest of that weekend. She spent all her time in Tim's car, and afterwards boasted that she'd got along so well, Tim thought she could soon take her driving test. 'But I need a bit more practice,' she said. 'You'll have to go out with me, mother. I just need someone with a licence to sit by me.'

Elaine said nothing. She didn't relish the prospect of trying to instil in Deborah the many requirements of driving a car.

The week before the party sped by. Elaine was cooking every evening, and Rachel bought Deborah a new trouser suit to wear. The invitations were sent out, though Deborah had not told Elaine whom she was inviting, just the numbers.

The Saturday was bright and cool. Elaine was up early putting the house to rights. They had an early lunch, and as they sat at the table in the kitchen, Deborah said 'It's my party, don't forget.'

'You mean,' Elaine asked, 'that you want me and Gran to keep out of the way, as usual.'

'That's right. Can't mix the generations. It never works.'

Elaine glanced at Rachel, who was smiling. 'Of course, dear. We understand. Try not to make too much noise. That's all we ask.' She was including Elaine in her own age group, and Elaine felt a stab of resentment.

'You seem able to mix generations with your guests,' she put in.

Deborah laughed. 'Oh, some are young for their age, aren't they? Especially men. They don't age like women do.'

Immediately Elaine felt old and bent and colourless.

The afternoon passed quickly. Elaine had to put finishing touches to trifles and complete last-minute savouries. She set out the coffee cups and made the percolator ready, so that Deborah had only to switch it on.

She glanced at the clock and realised that there was now only half an hour before the guests were due.

She would go upstairs and change, and sit in her room. She had a new library book to amuse her. She wondered, vaguely, where Deborah was. Probably prinking in front of her mirror with the new hair set she had had.

When she had dressed, Elaine sat near the bedroom window to watch for Andrew's taxi to arrive. Even if Deborah barred her mother from the party, Andrew would want to see Elaine, if only briefly. She had made up with extra care, and she wore a soft, angora sweater, that looked festive without being formal.

When the first guests, two girls from the secretarial college, rang the bell, Deborah seemed a long time letting them in. Elaine went to her daughter's bedroom and rapped smartly on the door. 'Your guests are arriving, Deborah. You must go and greet them. Don't leave them standing on the doorstep.' There was no reply.

Elaine opened the bedroom door, to find the room empty. Where had Deborah got to?

Elaine ran downstairs, admitted the two girls, who were shy and giggly, took their coats and put them into the sitting room, offering them a pile of records to choose from, and showing them how to set the record player going.

Then she left them and went to Rachel. 'Do you know where Deborah is?'

'She went to fetch Andrew.' Rachel answered complacently. 'Didn't you hear her get the car out?'

'Get the car out, but . . . ' Elaine hadn't heard the garage doors being opened, nor the car starting up. 'Has she gone alone? Or has Tim gone with her?'

'I don't know,' Rachel said. 'She says she can manage well enough now.'

'She's only breaking the law,' Elaine said bitterly, 'and Heaven knows what else. Andrew will be furious.'

At that moment there was the sound of a car door banging, and Elaine went to her own room to look down into the road. A taxi had drawn up. Deborah and Andrew were on the pavement. Deborah helped him along the short path to the front door. He was walking with a stick.

Elaine stayed where she was. People were coming quickly now. Let Deborah take care of them.

It wasn't long before there was a knock on Elaine's door. She opened it to find Tim on the landing. 'Mr. Nicholson says can he have a word with you — downstairs. He can't get up here very easily, so . . . '

Elaine nodded. 'Where is he?'

'In the dining room. The others are still in the sitting room.'

Andrew was standing by the window when Elaine came into the room with its shrouded table. He turned quickly. 'Hello, my dear.'

'Hello, Andrew. I hope you are much better.'

'Yes, I am. I shall be able to drive again when I've seen the doctor on Monday. I shall get back to the office then. But why did you let Deborah take my car out?'

'I didn't know about it, or I would have stopped her — or tried to. She's not easy to control.'

'Well, something ought to be done about her. It was a mad thing for her to do. She's a danger to herself and to everyone else.'

'She didn't . . . hurt anyone, did she?'

'Yes, me. By denting a wing, scraping the paintwork and generally behaving like a lunatic. She was trying to turn round in the gateway of the house across the road. I wouldn't let her bring the car back. We came by taxi.'

'I hope you told her what you felt about it. You have more influence than I have.' Elaine was withdrawn. This was the first time in weeks that she and Andrew had met, and here they were, embroiled in an argument over Deborah's behaviour.

She felt tears burning at the back of her eyes. 'Will the damage cost much to put right?'

'My insurance company will deal with that. But really, that girl is a menace. She had no L plates on and she was unaccompanied. She hadn't even driven the car before.'

'I know. And I'm very sorry. I'll try to . . .'

Andrew seemed to relent. 'Oh, forget her, Elaine. I haven't seen you for so long. You never called to see me, nor even enquired after me, so far as I can tell.'

'You were getting plenty of fuss. You didn't need me as well.'

'Didn't I? Let me tell you . . .' He

broke off as the door opened and Deborah came in.

'Oh, there you are, Andrew,' Deborah said. 'I missed you. We'll be starting to eat in a few minutes. What are you doing here, mother?'

Andrew's eyebrows went up. 'I was under the impression that she lived here, too.'

'Well, she can't be bothered with my parties, can you, mum? She likes to keep out of the way.'

'Likes to . . . at least she can eat with us. I expect she got most of it ready. Come on, Elaine, we'll get a head start.' He peeled the covers off the dishes of food and offered Elaine a plate.

She shook her head. 'No, thanks. Deborah doesn't want me to hang around. She says it cramps her style.'

'Then I'll go with you,' Andrew said. 'I'm too old for teenage fun.'

'No, Andrew,' Deborah protested. 'You've come to my party. If it gets too noisy for you, you and I will go off somewhere quiet by ourselves.' She went to him and took his hands.

Elaine slipped through the door just in time to avoid the press of young people in search of refreshment. She stayed in her room, and at midnight, she undressed and got into bed. The din downstairs was as loud as ever, and she knew she wouldn't sleep properly until the party was over.

She wondered how Andrew could stand it for so long. Or had he and Deborah gone to a quiet place, as the girl had promised.

At length Elaine dozed off, so that she never knew at what time the party ended.

The next morning Deborah was up early, and she was bright and cheerful. There was all the litter and disorder of the party to be cleared, and Deborah even helped by collecting glasses and emptying ashtrays.

Elaine did the washing up, and Deborah took up Rachel's breakfast to her. When she came downstairs again, Deborah hung about in the kitchen.

'Tim's going back this morning,' she said. 'He couldn't stay for the whole weekend.'

'Oh, what a pity.'

'Yes. He'd promised to take me out for some driving practice. Andrew says I mustn't go out on my own again. It would worry him. So . . .'

'Is he taking you himself?'

'Not yet. Not until he's back at the office. He says it would look bad. But he said I could have his car if you would sit by me. So that I could get some experience.'

'Oh, he said that, did he?' Elaine's answer was sharp with irritation. 'That I could sit by you?'

'In case I was stopped.'

Elaine stared at her daughter. 'Surely you can't trust me.'

'But there is no one else. I can rely on myself. It's just for the looks of the thing.'

Elaine swallowed her indignation. Did the girl realise how devastatingly rude she was? Yet, she knew that if she refused to go out with Deborah, her daughter would set out alone.

'Very well,' Elaine said. 'When I've finished here and we've had lunch, we could collect the car for an hour.'

When Rachel got up, she was annoyed to hear that the other two were going out. 'I'm always left on my own,' she complained. 'Nobody cares how lonely I am.'

'You could come with us,' Elaine said to pacify her.

'I think I will. It will be better than sitting here, worrying.'

'Very well. We'll bring the car here before we set off,' Elaine promised.

It was quite a long walk to Andrew's lodgings. He kept his car in a garage behind some allotments, and he had given Deborah a key. So it wasn't necessary to call at the house, although they had to drive past it to get to the main road.

When they came along the street, Andrew was waiting for them on the pavement, and Deborah drew up with a jerk.

'Steady,' he said. 'Treat a car gently. Like an animal, it's best tamed with kindness.'

Deborah laughed. 'I wish you'd take me yourself, Andrew. I could learn so much from you.'

'You have an excellent tutor, or I wouldn't trust you with my car, would I. Did we disturb you last night?' He had turned to Elaine.

'No. I went to bed.'

'And I got Tim to run me home. These young folk wear me out. I'm too old for parties.'

'What rubbish,' Deborah protested. 'You were the liveliest of the lot. Especially in that kissing game.'

He smiled. 'I have to make the most of my chances.'

'You can find plenty,' Deborah said cheekily, 'if you really want to.'

'Yes, if I really want to.' He was looking at Elaine, who turned her head away.

She tried hard not to be vexed by the clumsy flirting her daughter tried to indulge in. And she felt Andrew played up too much. Though it would be an unusual man who wasn't flattered by being so obviously pursued by an attractive girl. 'Come along, Deborah.' She spoke more briskly than she intended. 'There'll be no time for a lesson if we don't pick up your grandmother now.'

'Oh, a family affair,' Andrew remarked. 'You're brave to take on the pair of them, Elaine.'

She didn't answer, and Deborah let in the clutch too hard, so that the car lurched away.

'Take care of my property,' Andrew called after them.

'He means me,' Deborah said with a silly smirk.

Elaine quickly realised that Deborah's efforts at driving were in line with her temperament. She was aggressive and impatient, and indignant when Elaine reproved her, or tried to tell her what to do.

'When I need your help, I'll ask for it.

I'll learn for myself, thank you very much.'

Rachel sat in the back without speaking, but Elaine could feel the older woman's disapproval. She glanced back once at the taut mouth, the stiffly held body, then kept her eyes on the road.

It wasn't Rachel's way to be silent for long, and when she began to feel she was safe, she started her back-seat driving. 'Look out for that dog, darling. That's a nasty corner coming up. Take it carefully. Don't try to go too fast yet, Deborah, dear.'

Elaine could see that Deborah found these comments galling. The girl started to crash her gears, and to steer erratically. Elaine turned to ask Rachel to be quiet. 'You're putting her off. Please, don't divert Deborah's attention.'

At that moment the car lurched. Without knowing what was happening, Elaine pulled on the handbrake. 'Stop,' she yelled to Deborah. The girl, fortunately pushed out the clutch, and the car stopped with a shudder. They were within two feet of a car coming in the opposite direction. This car, too, had stopped.

The driver of the other car came and put his head through the window. 'You want to look out better than that. Are you supposed to be the experienced driver?' He looked at Elaine. 'It's your responsibility, you know. That could have been a nasty accident. Fortunately, I was able to stop. That girl needs watching.' He went back to his car, drove round them, and was off.

'Get the car back on to the right side of the road,' Elaine told Deborah. 'And be much more careful. If you do any more damage to Andrew's car . . . '

'*I* do damage. As that man said, it's all your fault. You should have been watching, instead of nagging at gran.'

'She's right. You're supposed to be the responsible one. I should have thought, after what happened before, you'd have been doubly careful to see that nothing more happened to Deborah. You're just careless, Elaine. You don't concentrate on what you're doing. And it's highly dangerous on the roads. If you haven't learned your lesson by now . . .'

'You shut up,' Elaine's voice was dangerously calm.

Deborah started the car and moved it to the proper side of the road, then she stopped again. She turned to her mother. 'I shall tell Andrew that you can't be trusted to look out for me. Then he'll take me himself, so that we'll both be safe, the car and me.'

Before she could stop herself, Elaine brought up her hand and gave Deborah a smart slap on the face. The girl's eyes widened in astonishment, then she opened her mouth to cry.

'Be quiet,' Elaine said. 'You said you didn't want my help. Now you're trying to blame me for your own carelessness. Just as you've always blamed me for your failings.'

Deborah was crying. 'I didn't want

your everlasting instructions, but it was your duty to look out for me. I should have known I couldn't rely on you. You know what daddy said you were with a car. I heard him say it. He called you a stupid fool. He called you that, just before . . . just before . . . a stupid fool, that's what he said.'

Deborah's crying dried up when Elaine opened the car door, got out and started to walk away. She moved quickly, until Rachel called after her. 'No. Don't go. You can't leave us here. Come back.'

Elaine stopped then, and walked slowly back. Rachel and Deborah were silent as Elaine took her seat again. She spoke in a low voice. 'You can drive slowly and carefully back to Andrew's garage. And then we will have done with driving lessons. I'm having no more of this. Do you hear, Deborah? And you, Rachel? I won't go through this again, not for anyone.'

Deborah shrugged, and started up as jerkily as ever. They dropped Rachel off

122

at her house, then Deborah drove, with exaggerated slowness, to Andrew's garage.

He had obviously been for a walk round the allotments, for he was standing, admiring some tulips, when they came along the driveway. Deborah put the car in the garage quite neatly, and Andrew came and shut the heavy doors for them. 'How did it go? All right?'

Elaine didn't answer his question, but said 'Thank you for lending us the car, Andrew. We shan't need it again.'

Andrew looked at Deborah, who burst out, 'It's all her fault. She never watched what I was doing. We might have had a smash. But she was too busy grumbling and turning to gran. You must take me out next time, Andrew. I'd feel safe with you.'

Elaine had started walking away.

'Not if your mother doesn't approve,' she heard Andrew say. Deborah stayed on to talk to him, and Elaine walked home alone.

6

Nothing more was said that week about driving a car. Deborah was sulking and Rachel was plotting.

Rachel kept glancing at Elaine, then looking away again. Elaine had seen the mannerism before. It meant that Rachel contemplated doing something that Elaine would disapprove of. But it was no use trying to guess what was in the older woman's mind.

Deborah and her grandmother whispered together sometimes, breaking off pointedly when Elaine came into the room. Elaine always tried not to mind when the other two shut her out. But it never ceased to hurt her. It was as though she were their enemy, their gaoler, and their rebuffs not only made Elaine unhappy, but suppressed the strong fount of affection that welled within her. She kept determinedly cheerful, and pretended not to notice.

Stan Davis asked her to work on the next Saturday morning. She didn't mind. The weekends always seemed long and barren.

She went to her office before Deborah and Rachel were up, and she worked hard until twelve o'clock, when Stan said she could go.

He had just come into the office, and he said, 'There's someone waiting for you outside. Cheeky devil. I've told him what I think about it.'

'About what?'

'About chasing you.'

'Nonsense,' Elaine murmured, but couldn't control the colour in her face, nor the tremor of the heart.

She took her time in getting ready, to give herself a chance to be calm and cool when she saw Andrew. He was sitting in his car and got out when he saw her emerge from the office door.

'Are you quite better?' she asked formally as she came towards him.

'Quite,' he said. 'And cheerful with it.

I've brought a picnic. Hop in.'

'Oh,' she stared at him. 'A picnic. Not for me, of course.'

'For you, you silly lady. Why do you never believe that I want just you? Well, this time I've got it all arranged.'

'Got what arranged? I'm sure you must realise that I can't go out this afternoon. I have too much to do at home, and they're expecting me home for lunch.'

'Oh no, they aren't. I've taken care of it, I tell you. I telephoned your mother-in-law and informed her that you wouldn't be back before this evening. And I gave her no fixed time to expect you.'

Elaine's eyes opened wider. 'What did she say?'

'She moaned a bit at first. Then she became rather coy, and guessed why I wanted to talk to you. I told her to let Deborah look after her. She said they had some shopping to do, and she wanted me to call in later, as there would be a surprise.'

'I shan't dare go home after this,' Elaine said as they both got in to the car. 'If you insist on a picnic, then we must make it a short one, and I will get back to them as soon as I can.'

He smiled at her and shook his head. 'We have to talk, you and I. And it may take a little time.'

She made no more protests, and he drove quickly away from the town. Eventually he took the road that followed the river, and they came to a small village that boasted an inn on the river bank.

'We'll eat our food here, then we'll go to the pub for a drink,' he said. 'Then we'll walk.'

She shrugged. 'You have it all worked out.'

'Of course. It's time someone took you in hand. Oh, Elaine, this is what I've been wanting. To get you to myself. We have so much to say to one another.'

She didn't reply, but started unwrapping the packages he had brought. They sat in the car to eat, because the day was chilly, in spite of its brightness. They watched the sunlight flinging silver spangles on the river.

Elaine felt at peace. She enjoyed having her life ordered by the man at her side. It gave her a feeling of relief and security. For a while, just for a little while, she would forget her responsibilities. He had arranged this. She would enjoy it.

She felt even the muscles of her face relax, and she exclaimed in delight when, after folding up the paper bags he suddenly produced a bunch of violets and presented them to her.

'Oh, lovely. Lovely,' she said, pressing the small bunch to her face. She smiled at Andrew happily, and he caught her to him. Her lips trembled under his, but she did not push against him. Instead, she rested in his arms, and put up a hand to caress his face. The violets were crushed between them. Then she pulled gently away, and sighed.

'I've wanted to do that for so long,'

Andrew said. He gave her a quick kiss on her forehead. 'I'll not rush things. We'll go for that drink now.'

After they had refreshed themselves at the inn, they set off, arm in arm, along the river bank. There were few people about. Just the occasional solitary fisherman.

'I'll talk first,' Andrew said at length.

'Must we talk?' she asked him. 'Can't we just enjoy this day?'

'This is only the beginning,' he assured her. 'We must know one another properly first. Let's sit down.'

He took off his macintosh and spread it on the grass. They sat close together, watching the river.

He started to speak. 'As I told you before, I've already been married. My wife divorced me. We had been apart the necessary number of years, so it was easy for her to get a divorce on the grounds of irretrievable breakdown. She's married since, and now has a little girl.'

Elaine glanced at him. This was a

bare outline of events, and told her nothing.

'Sheila and I,' he went on, 'married because we thought she was pregnant.'

Elaine felt herself stiffen, but tried not to draw away from him. He put an arm round her waist, as if to keep her near to him.

'My father was a doctor, but he had little to do with me. He was too busy looking after his patients. My mother died when I was ten, so I suppose I needed affection. At twenty-one I was as big a fool as anyone else at that age. Sheila was a year younger, and a bit over-eager.'

Elaine made as if to speak, but he hurried on. 'Oh, I'm not excusing myself, but it's true that Sheila made all the opportunities. Her mother was keen for her to be married. She was an only child, and her father was a postman. I suppose her parents thought of me as a a good 'catch'.'

He paused. 'Then when Sheila thought she was in the family way, as we used to say, we made quick arrangements to get married. I still hadn't served my articles, but her dad helped us. He was a good sort, and neither he nor her mother has ever reproached me. But we needn't have bothered.'

'What do you mean?' Elaine's voice was low.

'On our honeymoon Sheila told me it was a 'false alarm' and she'd learned how not to let it happen again. So we set up house together on my savings, and Sheila got herself a part-time job.'

'What was she like?' There was a wistfulness in the question.

'Quite pretty. And ambitious at that time. She was always on at me to take her to social events where she could meet 'people who mattered'. She felt that I, as a doctor's son, had contacts with people she could never have mixed with before. She sent out invitations, in the hope of getting them in return.'

Elaine sat quite still, so Andrew gulped and went on, 'I was still

131

studying and earning next to nothing. Entertaining was too costly for me, and I asked her to put the brake on. But she couldn't just sit at home at night whilst I swotted. She got mixed up with the set she admired — people who wore expensive clothes, ran expensive cars, lived in big houses, and drank expensive drinks at country clubs. It became that I hardly ever saw her. She'd go off at weekends, and I never knew with whom.'

'So it was all her fault?' Was Elaine's voice accusing?

'No, of course not. I just couldn't give her what she wanted, or thought she wanted. I suppose, if I had cared enough, I would have made a bigger effort to stop her — to keep her. But I just let things slide. I let her down. I was conscious of this. She got herself mixed up with a chap with a nasty reputation. I did blow my top at this, and I think that was all the poor kid wanted. For me to show I cared about her. But — I didn't. Not really. And I was to blame for marrying her.'

There was silence for a few moments. 'I think I can understand how she felt.' Elaine whispered at last. 'It is awful to offer love and have it thrown back in your face.'

Andrew looked at her appealingly. 'Yes. She hated me in the end. But she found the right man. He's an electrician and they live very happily in a council house. She dropped her ambitions, and found that all she really needed was true love and a family.'

'I'm glad she found them,' Elaine said. 'She paid pretty dearly for them.'

Again Andrew looked at her. 'I paid a bit, too. I wasn't very happy, tied to someone who . . . who . . . '

'She obviously had too much to give,' Elaine interrupted.

Andrew shrugged. 'Obviously, she has all your sympathy. And you think I was an unfeeling bounder.'

'No, I don't think that, Andrew.'

'What then?'

'That you were perhaps a little too

involved in your own affairs, and not able to realise the needs of your wife.'

He was silent then.

Elaine got to her feet. 'It's getting cold. Can we walk again?'

They moved away towards where the car was parked. The chill between them was not only in the air.

'Well,' Andrew said finally. 'Now you know about me. I said we would have to talk. It's altered your opinion of me.'

'Not really,' she answered. 'I'm glad you told me. Yes, I feel I know you better, and I liked the way you talked of your marriage. You weren't full of blame and bitterness, as some men would have been. I think that now you have lived a little longer, you would have much more understanding. You have learned to consider people more.'

He smiled ruefully. 'That's something I suppose. What I have learned is that I love you and want you. But you've made me feel unworthy of you.'

'Oh, Andrew.' Elaine stopped in alarm. 'God forbid that I should seem to be critical of your attitude or of your conduct. Who am I to pass judgement on anyone? I've made such a mess of my own life, that every story I hear of anyone else's, I try to analyse and find causes for. Perhaps, sub-consciously, I hope to be able to explain my own failure eventually.'

Andrew gave her a quick kiss, and they moved on again. 'Tell me about the accident,' he said. 'What happened and how?'

She seemed to shrink further into her coat. 'Please, Andrew,' her voice had diminished. 'You have been so frank with me, I know I owe it to you to try and be equally so with you, but . . . I can't. I can't talk about that. It's something that is with me all the time. I don't think anyone can realise what it is like to have been responsible for death — the terrible, everlasting pain of regret. It never goes away, or gets less.'

He took one of her hands. 'All right, darling. Perhaps some other time, when the circumstances are right. I know it would help you, if only you could talk. Especially to me. I love you, and want to make life more easy for you.'

She gave him a grateful glance. They had reached the car, and they sat in silence for a while, watching the slow-moving water of the river. It was a metallic grey now, and looked cold, powerful, menacing.

'Let's go,' Elaine said.

Andrew drove slowly through many riverside villages. At last they came to a small cathedral town, where the streets were hushed, and the few shops flourished apologetically.

Opposite the cathedral was an old, timbered inn, where they went and asked for tea. It was served in the lounge, empty and soundless, for the slight, natural noises of the building were stifled in the ancient hangings in the room. There was deeply upholstered furniture and a thick carpet. Even the firelight was noiseless, for it was electric.

Andrew and Elaine felt they had to

talk in whispers as they enjoyed the ample tea of sandwiches, scones, jam and cream and cakes. Elaine would have liked to linger in this slumberous atmosphere, but she glanced at her watch when she noticed that outside the daylight was fading.

'I must go back,' she said.

Andrew got up, making no protest. He paid the bill, and they went out into the street. 'Let's have a brief look round the cathedral,' he said.

They spent a little time under the high, vaulted roof of this beautiful building, which was now softly lit. Then Elaine went to stand before the altar. It bore a display of spring flowers that were enhanced by the warm, gentle glow that filled this place of dedication.

When Andrew came to her, tears were pouring down her face. 'My love, what is it?' he whispered.

'The vows we make,' she said. 'How dare we do it?'

Andrew drew her away and led her out of the cathedral and back to the car.

'Come now,' he said. 'Don't let our outing end like this. I wanted it to be a happy day for you. I know I spoiled it with my confessions . . . '

'Oh, no. Of course you didn't.' She put out a hand to him. 'I failed you, didn't I? You wanted sympathy and understanding, and I was taken up by the other side of the story. Selfishly so. I wanted to know what your wife had felt. Because she had disappointed you — just as I disappointed Michael. So perhaps I felt some of her guilt.'

'Guilt? Who can apportion blame? And how do you think you failed your husband?'

Andrew watched the outline of Elaine's face in the darkness of the car, and felt her appeal.

'I wasn't the wife he had wanted. He told me so. I was no good to him. I failed him in every way. Even with Deborah. He wanted a son. And then . . . and then . . . I killed him. He died after the accident, but I know it caused his death.'

'Oh, Elaine,' Andrew exclaimed. 'It sounds too one-sided. You, too, had your needs. Did he consider those? Did he disappoint you?'

She was very still. 'I should never have married him.'

'Why did you?'

'I thought I loved him. And I would have done, if he had let me. But you see, I couldn't please him. Not in any way.'

Andrew turned away from her. 'My God, you found a selfish one. I can gauge it from his mother, and from his daughter. They're the same breed. They take everything, but are responsible for nothing. They can always find someone to push the blame on to.'

Elaine suddenly shivered. 'All right,' Andrew said, starting the car engine. 'We've had enough for one day. I'll take you home now. But Elaine, I feel closer to you now that both of us have revealed ourselves to some extent. But you are so wrong, my darling. I must make you see it somehow.'

She didn't answer, and they were silent for most of the journey home. Andrew found a main road, so that they could move more quickly towards the town, and Elaine wondered, foolishly, if Andrew now wanted to be rid of her.

As they entered the lighted streets, she said, 'Please drop me at the end of the avenue, Andrew. Don't come to the house. I shouldn't like you to face the catechism that will be waiting for me.'

'But if I'm there, they won't do it.'

'Deborah will. She'll say I'm poaching on her preserves. You must disillusion her, Andrew, gently and kindly. I don't want her to be hurt unnecessarily.'

'Do that one good to suffer a little.'

'Oh no. She's had too much already for a young girl. The accident. Her limp. The loss of her father. No wonder she's difficult, and seems selfish. It's not fair that tragedy should have shadowed her young life.'

Andrew stopped the car at the end of the avenue, as she had asked. He was silent for a few moments. Then he took

Elaine in his arms and kissed her, delicately at first, then with growing demand, until she pushed him away. He felt the tears on her face. 'Damn,' he said. 'Oh, damn.'

Elaine opened the car door and slipped out. She waited until Andrew had driven away, then, before starting up the avenue, she paused to mop her face. She lifted her head, set her shoulders back and began to walk towards Rachel Barrington's house.

She saw a car standing in the drive outside, and wondered who was visiting them. She stopped again, under a lamp, and used its light to look at her face in her handbag mirror. She did what she hoped was a good repair job, and went on.

Strangely, there seemed to be no lights on in the house. As she opened the front door with her latch key, she saw a faint glow coming from the sitting room, which was at the back of the house. She went to the sitting room door, and was blinded by a torch being shone directly in her eyes.

'Don't move or make a noise.' The voice was cultured. 'Or I shan't hesitate to let you have this — in your face.'

Elaine put up a hand to shield her face. By looking through her fingers she could just discern the dark outline of a tall, slim man. She was rigid with fear, and felt sure the intruder must hear her heart beating.

The man didn't seem to know what to do next. 'Sit down,' he said after a long silence.

Elaine went to the nearest chair, and, trembling, lowered herself into it. She was less blinded by the glare here, and could dimly see that the writing desk was open and papers were scattered over the floor.

The man turned now to the desk, as if to continue his search. Then he was back, shining the torch straight at Elaine. 'Is there money anywhere else?' he demanded.

'There's practically none in the house,' she managed to answer. 'Not even any housekeeping money as it's the end of the month.'

The man hesitated. He didn't know whether to believe her or not, but dared not leave her for a further search. 'I'll have to make do with these.' He grabbed a pair of candlesticks which stood on the desk and Michael's silver cigarette box.

As he stuffed these things into a bag he was carrying, Elaine got up and took a step towards him. He turned in a flash and she felt wetness thrown on to the lower part of her face and on her neck and chest. The strong smell of ammonia stifled her.

The man pushed past her, knocking her on to the floor, and before she could get up, the overhead light was switched on. Deborah stood in the doorway.

The girl and the slim man faced one another. They stared in silence for what seemed a long time. Then Deborah spoke. 'Oh no,' she said. 'Not you.'

'Yes,' the man replied. 'Yes, Debbie, dear.'

Elaine pulled herself up and the man swung round to her. She had her hands over her eyes.

'What have you done to my mother?' Deborah demanded.

'She was being foolish, and if you don't behave, you'll get the same.'

'You can't frighten me,' Deborah retorted. 'I'll get the police.'

'Stay where you are.' The man's voice was louder now, more confident. 'Or I'll have a tale to tell them. About you and me, Debbie, and the good time we had together, and how I came here at your invitation, because you wanted to help me so that I could afford to make an honest woman of you . . . '

'Shut up,' Deborah said.

'You wouldn't like all that to come out in court, would you? As you know, Debbie, I can put up a good show when it suits me.'

'Deborah,' Elaine gasped. 'Do you know this man?'

7

'Of course she does,' the young man said. 'We had a lovely time together at my flat, didn't we, Debbie. Though I don't suppose you told your mother. It's not the sort of thing . . .'

'You rotten . . .' Debbie started.

'Shall I tell her?' the man mocked.

'I told her myself,' Debbie lied. 'She knows that I got away from you. She knows that nothing really happened.'

'That's what you say. But if I say different . . .'

'What is this man saying?' Elaine asked her daughter.

'He's just telling horrible lies, that's all. Lies. Oh, Tim.'

Tim's figure loomed in the doorway. 'What's going on here?'

'Nothing pal,' the burglar said. 'I'm just off. But don't ring the police. Debbie will tell you why.'

'Why you . . . ' Tim made a threatening move, but the slim man pushed past him and out of the front door, nearly knocking Rachel over as he went. 'Debbie. Debbie.' Rachel called. 'What's the matter?'

'I'll get on to the police,' Tim said going in the direction of the telephone. 'No, don't Tim,' Deborah stopped him. 'He told lies, but . . . '

Elaine went to her daughter, took an arm and shook her. 'What did he mean? You must tell me.'

Deborah glanced round at the three waiting faces. Elaine's eyes were red. Tim looked fierce and Rachel was frightened. The girl turned her head away.

Understanding dawned in Tim's face. 'Was he the chap you told me about?'

Deborah nodded.

'I wish I'd known, I'd have wrung his neck.' He turned to Elaine. 'Don't be upset. Deborah went out with him that day when we'd been riding, and he tried . . . '

Elaine spoke directly to her daughter. 'Tell me exactly what happened.'

Deborah hung her head as she told them of that Saturday afternoon.

'Are you sure you got away — in time?' Rachel wanted to know.

'Of course.' Deborah was indignant.

'That's what she told me the next morning,' Tim confirmed. 'I'm sure it's true . . .'

'But I don't want everybody to know about it,' Deborah said. 'If we had called the police . . .'

'Oh, my poor little love.' Rachel took her granddaughter in her arms.

Elaine went over to the desk. 'How much money was there in here?' she asked.

Rachel lifted her head. 'A lot. Two hundred pounds.'

'Two hundred . . . Where had it come from?'

'I drew it from my bank to pay for the car.'

'Car. What car?' Elaine was utterly bewildered.

'It's only a second-hand one,' Deborah said.

'And not much good,' Tim added.

'You shut up,' Deborah told him rudely. He shrugged.

'You were buying Deborah a car?' Elaine couldn't believe what she had heard.

'Well,' Rachel bridled. 'I had the money. She wanted — she needed a car of her own, so that she could drive it any time, and not have to keep asking other people. And I thought she might as well have use of my savings now, as wait until I'm dead.'

'Oh, Rachel,' Elaine sank into a chair. 'Two hundred pounds. The candlesticks. And the cigarette box. And he might come back for more.'

'He'd better not try,' Tim said. 'He wouldn't get away with it again. But I hope you realise that if you don't report the theft, you won't be able to claim on your insurance.'

'That's our affair,' Rachel put an arm protectively round Deborah. 'We don't want scandal. And no amount of money will let me have this child upset.'

Deborah started to cry. 'Shall we have to send the car back?'

'We'll have to see, lovie,' her grandmother tried to comfort her. 'We may have to wait a bit, but you shall have your car somehow. We're not going to let a horrible man like that spoil things for you. We'll see what we can do. Don't cry. Or you'll make me cry, too.'

Elaine closed her eyes, which were still smarting from the ammonia fumes. Was there no end to the old woman's foolishness? Rachel would sacrifice everything to get the girl that car. Everything and everybody. And Deborah might get tired of it even before she took her driving test. Oh, well, Elaine couldn't be bothered to worry about it now. Wearily, she pushed herself to her feet. She was weak-kneed and trembly. 'I'm going to bed,' she said. 'I'm tired.'

'Where have you been all day?' Deborah demanded before her mother reached the door.

Elaine turned and looked at her daughter. 'Never you mind,' she said, and closed the door behind her.

* * *

The next morning Tim came across before driving back to his college. He found Elaine in the kitchen alone. 'Are you all right, Mrs. Barrington? Were your eyes hurt last night? We ought to have had a look at them, but what with one thing . . . '

'They're all right, thank you, Tim. The ammonia didn't actually go into them. It was the fumes that made my eyes stream.'

'I thought you were jolly brave. You didn't even scream.'

Deborah, who had just come downstairs, heard the last remark.

'I expect Garry Leyland was as afraid as she was. And he didn't hurt her, did he?'

Tim went off and Deborah followed him to the front door, to say goodbye.

Elaine sighed. He was such a nice boy. Deborah didn't deserve him, and if she weren't careful, he would meet someone else, someone who admired him and was kind to him. What a silly girl, Deborah was. Almost as foolish as her mother had been all those years ago.

Remembrance of yesterday took over Elaine's mind. There had been so much else to worry about — the burglary and the car. Now Elaine sank into a kitchen chair, and pushed all thoughts aside except those of Andrew. Andrew who had looked to her for support and comfort when he had told her of his marriage, and whom she had so clumsily let down.

Had her own failure blinded her to everything but similar failures in others? The girl had married Andrew under false pretences, and because he was not the person his wife had hoped, she had gone off at a tangent, leaving him alone whilst she enjoyed herself with any comer. If Andrew had been a little blind, the girl had been very much so.

And, at least, she now had happiness, which still evaded the man she had cheated.

Elaine's impulse was to ring up Andrew, to tell him she realised she had been unkind, unthinking, that she now understood. He had made light of his unhappiness, put the blame on himself, and tried to explain the situation in a reasonable, decent way.

It was Elaine who had been filled with bias — just because the girl was another wife whose marriage had not given her what she wanted.

Elaine got up and looked out of the kitchen window at the untidy garden. Suffering made one selfish. Whether the pain was mental or physical. It wasn't true that unhappiness was ennobling. Just the opposite. It made one greedy for all one fancied one had missed. Elaine wanted love. Not the imperfect sort that had been between her and Michael. But some lasting love that could encompass all her weaknesses, all her misgivings.

Deborah went past the window. Elaine sighed. How could she find anything to blame in the girl? She was spoiled, yes. But she had courage. She had come through her ordeal with that awful man without disgracing herself. She had realised her own stupidity, and got herself out of the scrape without whining about the hurts she had sustained. Elaine felt some pride in that.

Rachel came to the kitchen door. 'We've got to keep that car,' she said. 'The child mustn't be disappointed just because that ruffian chose to break in here.'

To Rachel's astonishment, Elaine nodded. 'Yes, you're right. We must try and help her to keep this new interest. That man shan't spoil it for her. I'll draw out my savings certificates. And perhaps I could sell something — one of the rings my mother left me.'

'Oh, I have a bit left in the bank,' Rachel said. 'We can manage it between us.'

Andrew rang Elaine at the office the next morning. 'Are you all right?' he demanded, detecting something reluctant in her voice.

She hesitated to tell him about the burglary, for he would think her foolish to let the man get away because of his threat to Deborah. So she merely said they had lost some money, which they had put aside to pay for a second-hand car for Deborah.

Andrew became indignant. 'What car? Surely you aren't mad enough to pay for and run a car for that girl. Just because she fancies herself as a driver. She's a greedy little . . . '

Elaine stopped him. 'She's my daughter. Now I have a lot to do. I can't talk any longer.'

'Damn it all, woman,' Andrew exploded. 'Why must you always put me off? Can't we discuss your problems like sensible adults? If you expect me to stand by and see you exploited . . . '

'Goodbye,' she said firmly, angry and a little ashamed at her own weakness.

Maybe it was silly to gratify her daughter, but she couldn't go back on her word.

At lunch time Elaine went to the post office for a form of withdrawal for her savings certificates that she had acquired slowly over the months. She had tried to build a nest-egg to be used only in an emergency. Getting a car for Deborah didn't come under that category. Still, she had said she would do it. But was the car worth it? It must be checked before Deborah used it.

Andrew came into the office that afternoon to see Stan Davis about the accounts. He managed to spin out the visit until five o'clock, and came out of Stan's office as Elaine was putting on her coat.

'I suppose you won't refuse a lift home,' he said with some sarcasm.

'No. Thank you very much.' Elaine was polite. 'I want to be home early.'

'About that car,' he said. 'I don't suppose you've bothered to get advice about it. I'd better give it the once-over.

155

Come along, we'll need to get there before dark.' Was this his way of apologising for his outburst? Indicating that he would help in spite of his disapproval.

He drove in silence through the peak-hour traffic, and Elaine, who longed to tell him of her thoughts and regrets of yesterday, found herself unable to say anything.

'Good lord, is that it?' Andrew said when they drew up outside the Barrington house.

Deborah came running out. 'Oh, Andrew, I haven't seen you for ages. Where have you been all this time?' She threw her arms round him and held up her face for a kiss. He gave her a peck on the forehead. 'I see you've won again,' he said, and Deborah pouted.

'Let's have a look at this banger,' Andrew said practically. He lifted the bonnet and fiddled inside. Then he sat in the car and tried the controls. He backed the car on to the road for stopping and starting. The brakes

156

squealed every time he stopped.

He brought the car back into the drive, got out and measured the tread on the tyres.

'Well,' Deborah demaned. 'Isn't it all right?'

'Not to my satisfaction. You need one new tyre, the brakes must be adjusted, and the steering isn't tight enough. I'll get my garage to go over it and make it absolutely safe.'

'Will you? Oh, bless you, darling Andrew,' Deborah was ecstatic. 'Will you take me out in it then?'

'I might. If you behave yourself.'

Elaine, watching them together, wondered how and when the strong, but different kinds of love she had for these two creatures would ever be reconciled.

Andrew refused to join them for an evening meal, and Deborah watched him drive away. 'Isn't it good of him to have the car overhauled.'

'We shall have to pay for it,' Elaine reminded her. 'And there is still the licence and insurance. You must try and do your share,' she added tardily.

'Gran will see to it,' Deborah said confidently.

Andrew kept his promise, and the next day a garage hand collected the car and put trade plates on it for the journey.

That evening Rachel tackled Elaine. 'I never asked you about your outing with Andrew Nicholson last Saturday. I was amazed, I can tell you, when he rang up and told me you were spending the afternoon together. And you'd never said a word about it.'

'I didn't know myself.'

'What did he want? To ask about Deborah?'

'No.' Elaine answered briefly.

'Of course I didn't tell Deborah. She would have been upset. I was a bit myself. I haven't spoken of it before because of the burglary and the business of the car. But I think I should have an explanation.'

'An explanation! Why should I have to give an explanation?'

'Because he was Deborah's friend first.'

'Well,' Elaine found herself blushing. 'Deborah will have to realise sometime that . . . '

'That what?'

'That Andrew is too old for her. That his attraction for her is because she needs a father.'

Rachel struggled to her feet. Her face was crimson. 'Don't you dare to tell me that you are thinking of putting someone else in my Michael's place. That you have your claws in Andrew Nicholson. I'll not let you. He's Deborah's. She needs him. But not as a father. She needs an older man for stability and security, but not to replace the father you have denied her. No, I won't stand by and see her made more unhappy . . .' Rachel's voice started to tremble. 'I've had to watch her suffering, and I've suffered myself, but you shan't do that to her. Not while I have a breath in my body.' She clutched her breast. 'Oh, my heart,' she muttered.

Elaine went to her and lowered her into a chair. Then she fetched the brandy bottle and gave her mother-in-law a stiff dose, before she helped the older woman up to bed.

Elaine was shaken by Rachel's outburst. How would she ever be able to tell Michael's mother that Andrew had proposed to her, that she loved him and wanted to be his wife? She had felt that, if she waited, Deborah would tire of her hero worship and resign herself to a different relationship with the man she now imagined she loved.

But Rachel. She wouldn't change. She would create all the difficulties she could, in the hope of depriving Elaine and gratifying Deborah.

Elaine tossed in her bed that night. It was all too ridiculous. Why should an old woman and a young girl be able to spoil any prospect of happiness for two mature people? Because she had deeply wronged those two, her conscience reminded her. How could Elaine ever be happy again, remembering, as she must, that the old woman had lost a son and the child had lost a father.

And yet — and yet . . . it hadn't been her fault. Deep within her, whilst accepting the guilt, she knew it hadn't really been her fault. Was it fair that she should be paying for ever for a sheer accident? For ever and ever.

The next evening, when Elaine came home from the office, she was, for some reason she couldn't explain, relieved to see the drive to the house still empty. The car hadn't yet been returned.

Rachel told her different, when Elaine got into the house. 'The car came this afternoon. Deborah's taken it to try out. Just round the nearby roads. She won't be long.'

Elaine bit her lip. 'Why did you let her do it? There is no licence. No insurance. And she's a learner driver without supervision. She's breaking about every rule in the book. It's sheer madness.'

'But she was so anxious to try it on the road. It's only child-like. She won't do any harm.'

161

'She should have been stopped,' Elaine repeated, too angry to reason with her mother-in-law. 'Why is it she thinks there are rules for everybody else, but not for her? She's got the idea that she's too special to be limited like other people. That's what you've done for her, Rachel, given her a sense of importance that can only get her into trouble. You've ruined her as a person. Oh, if only I could afford to live in my own house, and bring her up myself.'

'How dare you. How dare you say that to me,' Rachel's face was contorted. 'After what you've done to my son's child. I've only tried to make up for what she has had to miss. She has no father, and I have no son. Deborah and I need one another, and I'll go on doing all I can for her, whether you like it or not. You shan't come between us. You shan't.'

The sound of a car door being slammed interrupted the argument, and Elaine ran outside. Deborah had brought the car into the drive. She was standing in front of it, looking at some damage on the front near-side wing.

'Now what has happened?' Elaine snapped at her.

'Nothing much. I just caught the wing. It can be straightened easily enough. Andrew will see to it for me.'

'And do you think Andrew will be pleased to hear that you've taken out the car without tax and insurance and without supervision. What are you trying to do, Deborah?'

'I don't know what you mean. Oh, don't kick up such a fuss. What's a bit of damage like this? It happens to everyone.' Deborah stalked indoors leaving her mother to stare at the bent wing with a feeling of sick despair.

They had a silent supper, and Deborah went off upstairs immediately afterwards. Rachel announced that she was going to rent a television set for herself, one that she could have in her room, and watch the programmes she liked from her bed, when she was tired.

Elaine took little notice of this talk,

and Rachel, too, took herself off, leaving Elaine to wash up the supper dishes and tidy round the house.

She was still working in the kitchen, when there was a sharp rap on the front door. Two tall policemen stood outside. Elaine's hand went to her throat. 'What is it?' she asked.

'May we come in?' the broader policeman said. Elaine stepped aside automatically, and nodded towards the sitting room. The men went in, but refused her invitation to sit down.

'That car outside,' one policeman began. 'Is it yours?'

Elaine nodded.

'Have you a licence for it? Is it insured?'

She shook her head. 'Not yet,' she whispered.

'You realise this is serious, don't you? Taking out an unlicensed, untaxed car.'

'Yes, I suppose so.'

'We've had some trouble in tracing it. It's still registered in the name of the previous owner, and we had to find your name and address from the garage that supplied it to you.'

Elaine stared at the men.

The other one spoke now. 'The police will prosecute, of course. The old man said he wouldn't lodge a complaint, as he didn't want a fuss. But unless you pay for the damage to his cycle . . . Fortunately, he wasn't hurt beyond a scratch or two, so you're lucky there. It might have been very serious. It's up to you to see him right.'

Elaine sank into a chair. She was trembling, and daren't speak.

'I suppose you were the driver,' the first policeman said, as an afterthought. 'The old man said it was a woman.'

Elaine looked up at him. He was scowling. She nodded.

'Name?' he demanded. 'And age.'

She muttered the words.

'Right.' The policeman finished writing. 'You'll be hearing from us.' The two men went out, their footsteps heavy on the thin carpet, and they banged the front door behind them.

Elaine sat for a long time, stunned, unable to move.

'Mummy,' Deborah stood inside the door, her face white and frightened. 'I couldn't help it. He wobbled and I just caught his back wheel. He bent my wing.'

'Did you stop?'

'No. I didn't want him to see me. How did they know about it — the police?'

'So you heard.' Elaine got up stiffly. 'Someone must have made a note of the car number.'

'What's going to happen. Mummy, I'm frightened.'

Elaine stared hard at her daughter, then her vision blurred. Deborah was still a child. A spoiled, head-strong child, but her child. Elaine's and Michael's. She felt again the young arms clinging to her when she comforted a younger Deborah. Deborah. Her baby.

'Don't worry,' she spoke chokingly. 'They think I did it.'

Deborah threw herself at her mother. 'Oh, darling. Bless you. Bless you. You can cope better than me. I daren't go into court again. I was so frightened last time, when I was only a witness. But you've been summoned before, so you . . .'

'Yes,' Elaine spoke bitterly. 'I've been through it before.'

'We'll help you,' Deborah promised. 'If they make it a big fine, we'll all save like mad, and . . . will they send you to prison?'

Elaine suddenly hardened against her daughter. 'Heaven knows. But this I can tell you. That blasted car goes back. The money we've drawn to pay for it can be kept towards whatever this business costs us, after we've paid for a new bicycle for the old man. You'll go and see him, Deborah. Tell him how sorry we are. Make sure he isn't hurt. And make it up to him. You'll do that, my girl.'

Rachel came in, complaining and tremulous. 'What's all the noise about?

What's happening?'

Elaine walked away, leaving Deborah to tell what story she liked to her doting grandmother.

8

Elaine felt that, at all costs, Andrew must not know of this last foolish impulse to save her daughter. Foolish? Perhaps, but natural. It was a parent's instinct to save a child from an ordeal, even an ungrateful, unloving child. An instinct too strong to be denied.

But Andrew would never understand this. He had no child of his own. He would be angry and blame Elaine, and she didn't think she could bear it. Better to finish with Andrew now than to go on being torn in two.

Deborah had the greater claim. As Elaine had tried to make Andrew understand, there was no room in her life for anything that could sever the tenous thread that held mother and child together. If Elaine had to choose between the two of them, she must choose the weaker, the one who had most need. And at that moment, it was Deborah.

And so Elaine avoided Andrew. She told Rachel and Deborah to say nothing to anyone about the court case, and they were more than ready to agree. When Andrew telephoned Elaine was brusque and made excuses not to see him. He called at the house several times, and she went to her bedroom and wouldn't come down. When he came to the office, she was so coldly formal that even his warm regard was quenched.

Eventually he became discouraged or disgusted, and he left all of them alone.

The summons came, and the date of the hearing was given as three weeks ahead. During that time Elaine lived through the earlier hearing again and again. Then there had been injuries, followed by death, and her own ordeal had seemed as nothing, the fine and the endorsement of her licence a mere formality. Any punishment had been, as the magistrates had said, in her anxiety about Deborah and Michael.

Even when Elaine had been told that Michael would have died in any case, she still blamed herself. The doctor tried to assure her that she had not even cut his life short. The accident had done no more than bruise and scratch him. The real cause of his death was a brain tumour that had gone undetected until the accident, when it was too late. If it had happened earlier, there might have been a chance.

Naturally, Rachel Barrington hadn't believed this, She felt that Elaine had killed Rachel's son as surely as if she had put a knife in his heart. And there was still Deborah and her lame leg.

As so often happens, the date of this new hearing was postponed. This was repeated three times, so that the time of waiting stretched itself over the months.

Small things filled Elaine's life. When no bill came from Andrew's garage for the repairs to the old car, Elaine rang the manager, and asked him about the charges. Reluctantly, he gave her the details, and she sent Andrew a cheque without a covering note. It came back, torn in half, and with no comment.

The car was taken back by the firm from whom it had been bought. They had little objection, as they had gained a free overhaul for it, and would sell for a better price.

The old man who had been knocked from his cycle, was given a new one, and the rest of Elaine's money and of Rachel's had to be put aside for the fees of a lawyer, as Elaine had no insurance to cover this cost for her.

The man she chose didn't seem very interested in the case. 'It should be pretty straightforward,' he said. 'You'll be fined, of course. And maybe banned for a while. Especially as this is your second offence.'

The lawyer wanted to know why Elaine had taken the car out, and she had to concoct a story about needing something urgently from the shops, and not being able to leave the house for long.

'Hmm, it's pretty thin,' the lawyer said. Elaine found that 'pretty' was one of his favourite words.

Eventually, Elaine decided that she would have to mention the matter to Stan Davis, as she would have to have time off to attend the hearing. His eyebrows went up at the story. 'Not like you, Elaine. Silly thing to do. Especially after the last lot. Anyway, don't worry. If the fine's too much for you, I'll lend you what you need.'

Elaine tried to thank him. He was a tough and demanding employer, but he was generous.

The day of the court case came at last. Elaine dressed and made up carefully, for her lawyer had impressed on her that appearances counted for a lot. She insisted that Rachel and Deborah should stay away.

She was called into court, and went to sit where she was told, without seeing anyone around her. She looked towards the bench. There were three magistrates, two women and a man.

Elaine felt her heart slide. She would have preferred two men and one woman.

After a while, she let herself look round the court and at the people sitting on the public benches. She felt the colour flood her face. Andrew Nicholson was gazing at her steadily. There was no readable expression on his face, no hint of concern or friendliness.

Elaine turned her head away. How had he got to know about this, and why had he come?

She was directed to the witness box, took the oath and mechanically answered the questions that were fired at her. She knew she was putting up what her lawyer would call 'a pretty poor show.' She felt she couldn't be bothered any more. Let them do as they wished.

If she went to prison, there might be some peace somewhere for her. She would have to work hard, but probably not more so than at present. In fact there might be more opportunity for reading and writing and painting, which she had once so much enjoyed.

But no one except Deborah, had suggested there was any chance of going to prison, and the penalty was as her lawyer had forecast. She was fined fifty pounds and her licence was suspended for a year. She turned away, feeling she had been let off lightly.

Elaine hurried to the ladies' cloak-room, and wasted time there. She wanted to give Andrew the opportunity of leaving without seeing her. Then she went to pay her fine on the spot. It gave her some satisfaction that she had enough money to hand over.

She was glad to walk out of that grey, echoing building, with its many small courts, where offenders were called to answer for their crimes. As she came down the steps, she saw that Andrew was waiting for her. He did not speak, but put a hard grip on her arm, and led her towards his car.

She could not resist him physically under the eye of the policeman who guarded the entrance to the court-house.

Andrew unlocked the off-side door of the car, and sharply pushed her into the passenger seat.

'There's no need to be rough,' she rebuked him.

He still said nothing as he took the driving seat, and drove quickly, almost recklessly, out of the town. Elaine made no more protest, but waited until they drew up outside a country inn. 'We'll get some food here,' he spoke at last. 'Then we'll talk. Come on.'

She stayed where she was. 'Come on,' he repeated, his voice cold and commanding.

She shook her head. 'I couldn't eat with you in that mood. I'll stay here until you've had your lunch.'

He sighed heavily, as though trying to keep a hold on his temper. 'Then we shall neither of us eat. And I'm hungry.'

It was Elaine's turn to sigh. Slowly she got out of the car, and followed Andrew into the inn.

They had slices of beef off a great joint, and the landlady served the vegetables. The second course was apple pie, followed by cheese and biscuits. To her own surprise, Elaine found that she was able to eat heartily. And she enjoyed the coffee and liqueurs that finished off the meal.

Andrew spoke as little as possible as they ate, and they both concentrated on the good food. Elaine felt herself content and mellowed as they went out to the car.

Still speaking little, Andrew drove away from the village, and stopped in a quiet lane between high hedges. He backed into a field gate opening.

Deliberately, he turned to Elaine. 'Now tell me about this latest foolishness. I'm certain it wasn't you in the car that day. It must have been Deborah. Why didn't you let her take the rap? Is she to be cocooned in cotton wool all her life? She has to grow up sometime, and face up to the consequences of her own actions. You're doing her no service by all this sheltering. In fact, just the opposite. It will come all the harder for her when she has to take on responsibility for herself.'

He was using all the arguments that Elaine had dreaded to hear. 'She is my daughter,' she murmured. 'And I did cripple her. And whatever she may seem to you, I love her. I had to do all I could for her.'

Andrew was silent for a few moments, then he went on remorselessly. 'I want to know all about that first accident. Until I know, I can't reconcile your attitude to Deborah and Rachel. I'm willing to bet that you had little blame. Tell me about it, Elaine. Please. We can't get things straight between us until I know all about your background.'

The feeling of well-being drained away from Elaine. Andrew wanted her to re-live that horror, as she had been doing through the last few weeks. And she wanted to forget it. Not to talk about it ever again.

He wouldn't believe her, anyway.

Why should he? Rachel hadn't. Nor the lawyer. Nor anyone. Not even Michael, and he was there. She looked at Andrew, who was carefully watching her. She knew he wouldn't leave her alone until she had told her story. 'All right,' she sighed. 'I'll tell you what I can.'

'Go on,' he said tensely.

'We were going on holiday, Michael, Deborah and I. Rachel had wanted to come, but I asked Michael not to bring his mother. And, for once, he gave in. We lived with his mother then, of course, and I think he was tired of her everlasting nagging, too. So the three of us set off. I drove, Michael sat beside me, and Deborah in the back.

'Deborah hadn't wanted to go without her grandmother, who would have treated her to everything she wanted. But Michael told Debbie that she couldn't have her own way all the time. They were both rather bad-tempered, and I was wondering what sort of a holiday it was going to be.

'Michael criticised my driving, as he criticised everything I did — my cooking, my gardening, my — even my loving. Because he was ill-tempered, his comments were sharp, and he made me nervous. I asked him to take over, but he said he needed a rest.

'Deborah, in the back, was wanting to take all our attention, and when I ignored her, she grabbed my arm suddenly, and half pulled me round to face her. I lost control of the car, and we ran into a tree.

'Michael bumped his head. I held on to the wheel. Deborah, who had been standing up, was thrown over the seat, and caught her leg between the seats as she went. I heard it break, and she was screaming with pain. Michael was dazed. I saw an A.A. box down the road. I got out and ran to it, and called an ambulance.'

Elaine stopped talking for a moment. She was trembling. Then she forced herself to go on. 'It seemed at first that Deborah was the only one seriously hurt. Her leg was badly torn as well as broken. Then Michael developed headaches. It was a brain tumour and he died of it.'

'So you didn't kill him.'

'They said not. But I've always felt . . .'

'Or Rachel has always blamed you, and Deborah took her cue from her.'

'Maybe so.' Elaine felt drained now. She started to weep quietly. Andrew took her in his arms. 'I can see that you, being you . . . Oh, these Barringtons. First Michael. Then Rachel. Then Deborah. Well, it's over now. You must rest with a quiet mind. It was Deborah who took the car out without licence or insurance, wasn't it? Not you.'

Elaine nodded. It was no use trying to keep things from Andrew any longer. All she could do was beg him to be quiet about it. To leave her alone, because she couldn't marry him, not with the responsibilities she still had. No matter how he tried to persuade Elaine that she had no blame, Rachel and Deborah still depended on her, and she couldn't desert them. Not just to achieve her own happiness. There could be none for her, knowing she had failed them.

Andrew was quiet for a long time. 'I'll take you home, Elaine,' he said eventually. 'You'll have to decide now, with whom you want to live. With your daughter and mother-in-law. Or with me. I have a feeling that I might lose, unless I can persuade you. Oh, Elaine, I need you so.'

'So do they.'

'I've gone through hell these last few weeks, when you made it so plain you couldn't stand having me near you. Then I found out why from Stan Davis. You were afraid I wouldn't let you go through with this — this charade. And you were right. I wouldn't. Now, it's too late. But you still have to decide. If you don't marry me, both our lives are lost — in the sense of being wasted. If you do, Rachel and Deborah might be upset for a little time, but they would adjust.'

'But they are . . . helpless,' she answered.

Andrew took her in his arms, and she felt the relief and comfort of being held by him. She was eager for his kisses, and she clung to him as if she could never let go. She almost felt the leap of his blood, the urgency of his need. Reluctantly, she pushed him away. This was not for her. 'I can't,' she whispered, and she felt his arms go slack.

'All right,' he muttered. 'If that's your answer. I can't go on like this. If you won't have me . . . '

She felt a stab of fear at his words. If she refused him, he would turn elsewhere. Of course. So he should. His present life was arid. He needed a home. She swallowed on the pain that filled her. 'I understand,' she said.

He looked at her, then started the car. She powdered her nose as they drove along, trying to hide her face. She made no demur when he headed for the town.

He opened the car door for her when

they reached Rachel Barrington's house. She got out and waited as he drove away. They had no more words for one another.

'That really is the end,' she told herself. The pain must give in time. She wouldn't always feel so bereft, so deep in sorrow. She tried to compose her face before she went into the house.

Rachel was reading the newspaper. 'It could have been worse,' she said. 'A good thing you had enough for the fine.'

'There's still the lawyer's bill,' Elaine reminded her.

Deborah came in late that night. Rachel and Elaine were in bed. The girl came to her mother's room, knocking timidly, and waiting for permission before she entered.

Deborah stared at her mother for a moment. Then she burst out. 'I'm sorry, mummy. I'm ever so sorry.' Elaine's face crumpled at those childish words. She held out her arms, and Deborah went to her. As she held her daughter close, Elaine told herself that this was sufficient reward. This made everything worthwhile. Her daughter had come back to her.

But Deborah's new attitude didn't prevail for long. She was soon back to normal, resentful and demanding. She waited triumphantly one evening for Elaine to come home from the office. The girl hardly allowed her mother to get through the door before she pounced. 'Andrew rang me up a little while ago. He wants to see me again. So you see — you were wrong.'

'Wrong?'

'You thought I was too young for him. I even think you imagined he fancied you. Well, he's left you severely alone lately, and now he wants to see me.'

'Where and when?' Elaine asked in a low voice.

'He wants to come here. So, I wondered, could you keep out of the way for a bit? He wants to come tomorrow evening.'

'Very well,' Elaine said. 'I have to work overtime tomorrow in any case. And I can call at the library. Will that be all right?'

'I suppose so. But don't hurry. Andrew's coming at about seven.'

Elaine puzzled all the evening over Andrew's motive in seeing Deborah. It wasn't, of course, as Deborah supposed, but it wasn't Elaine's task to disillusion her. Andrew must do it himself. Was that why he wanted to talk to the girl?

The next day, the thought of Andrew's visit to see Deborah interrupted Elaine's concentration. She made a lot of mistakes in her typing, and her letters took much longer than usual to dispose of. So she had a legitimate excuse to stay late.

Stan Davis drove her hard, but she was glad of the many small bonuses he included in her pay packet when she had been extra busy. This time he demurred. He insisted on locking up at seven o'clock, saying that Elaine looked dead tired.

As she had promised, she went to the library, and lingered over the magazines. But soon this place started to empty. It was time to close.

Elaine went out into the street. The shops were shut, and it was chilly to be window gazing. A sudden impatience made up her mind. Why should she be barred from her own home? She would go in very quietly, and up to her room to bed. They probably wouldn't even hear her. As Stan had noticed, she was very tired.

She took a 'bus, then walked slowly along the avenue. There was a light in the front room of the house. So Deborah had chosen to entertain Andrew in the dining room. Presumably, Rachel would be watching television in the sitting room.

Elaine put her key into the lock carefully and quietly, and pushed the door open. As she stepped into the hall, she was enveloped by voices — Andrew's deep and angry, Deborah's shrill in protest, Rachel's wailing.

Elaine listened for a moment and could make nothing of the clamour. She went into the dining room.

The three of them were standing up. Andrew was on the hearthrug. Rachel was near the door, as if she had just come in. Deborah stood near the window, gripping the back of a chair. They were all silenced when Elaine entered.

She looked questioningly at them one by one, but no one spoke. She drew off her gloves and sat down. 'Will someone please tell me what has been going on?'

They all started together. 'Oh, mummy,' Deborah said loudly. 'Andrew's been absolutely horrid to me. He says I'm selfish. I'm not, am I? I didn't ask you to . . .'

Rachel's voice took over. 'Don't let this man ever come near my house again. I won't stand by and let him bully that child. He must be mad. Get away from us, Mr. Nicholson, and don't ever come back.'

Andrew tried to take Elaine's hand,

but she drew it back. 'Shut up, all of you,' she said. 'Let me hear what you have to say one at a time. Now, Andrew. Why did you come here tonight?'

'I came to ask your daughter to be reasonable. I told her we loved one another, and wished to marry, and she went off like a fire-cracker, so I gave her a few home truths. Then this lady came pushing in with her abuse.'

Elaine turned to Deborah, who rushed on. 'He pretended he wanted to see me, then he said you and he were doing a line, and, naturally, I went off the deep end. I mean, it's not decent, is it — with a woman of your age. Besides, he'd been stringing me along, and I'd got to like him. But he was brutal. Said ghastly things. So I hate him now. How you could let him near you! Haven't you any self-respect?'

Elaine sighed and looked at Rachel, who had tears on her face. 'He's trying to break up our home, Elaine. You won't desert us, will you? I mean, after all, you owe something to both of us.

The child needs you until, until . . . and I can't be left alone, not just so that you can go off with him. You wouldn't be so selfish, would you? Not after all you've done . . .'

Elaine go up. 'Stop it, all of you. I'm sick of it. I'm sick of being badgered and nagged at and told what I must do. You're like a pack of hounds, tearing a fox to pieces. I tell you, I've had enough. Yes, even of you, Andrew. I'm going to leave you to it, until you can get yourselves sorted out. Goodnight.'

She moved quickly out of the room and through the hall. They came after her and watched as she went upstairs. She locked her bedroom door whilst she did some hasty packing.

They were still in the hall when she came down with her suitcase.

Andrew stepped forward. 'This is ridiculous, Elaine. Where could you go at this time of night? Please, darling, don't be silly.'

She pushed him aside, and picked up the telephone and rang for a taxi.

'You mean it then,' Deborah said, subdued. Rachel was crying. 'How could you? How could you? You're a cruel woman, Elaine. I always felt you were, but Michael would have you. I never liked you, and I didn't want him to marry you, though I never said a word to let you know how I felt.'

'You didn't have to,' Elaine said bitterly. 'And you can be quiet,' she said to Deborah who had started to cry as well.

Elaine turned to Andrew, and spoke stonily. 'We were all right until you came into our lives. Now, perhaps, you'll leave us alone, having upset all of us thoroughly.'

Andrew didn't answer, and Elaine flinched at the expression in his eyes.

There was a long, miserable silence. Elaine wished Andrew would go, but he stayed on until he heard the horn of the taxi. Then he opened the door and carried Elaine's suitcase to the taxi for her. He hung about as she got into the cab, so she told the driver to go to the centre of the town. She didn't want Andrew to hear her destination. He stood on the pavement, watching, as the taxi drove away.

Elaine decided to stay at a hotel. She chose the smallest she knew of, but of course, even this was expensive. She was in a mood of recklessness, and she was tired, utterly and entirely exhausted, both bodily and mentally.

9

Elaine had a talk with Stan Davis as soon as he came into the office the next morning. She made him promise that he would not tell Andrew Nicholson anything about her, where she was staying, when she might be leaving work.

Furthermore, he must let her know whenever Andrew was due to come to Stan's office. If he came unexpectedly, she would immediately leave.

Stan scratched his head as he listened to her orders. 'Have you two quarrelled?' he asked mildly. 'Well, it suits me. I never did like him chasing you.'

Elaine felt like hitting her boss, but she tackled her work in a more cheerful mood.

She was tempted several times to ring up Rachel, to find out how she and Deborah were faring, but she resisted.

Rachel spoke to Stan one morning, and Elaine heard him declare that he had no knowledge of Rachel's daughter-in-law. Rachel had evidently asked if Elaine was still in his employ, and he spluttered and stammered about being able to rely on nobody these days. Then, hastily, he rang off.

Elaine had to smile at his red, indignant face. 'I don't know why I have to be mixed up in your private life,' he complained. 'I suppose I'll have to put up with it. You're too useful to lose, but you're becoming a hard woman, Elaine.'

'I have reason to,' she answered.

'I saw Nicholson in the pub last night. He doesn't often drink, but he was tossing it back all right.' Stan glanced slyly at Elaine, to see the effect of his words. 'Talking to a blonde, as far as I can remember. Seemed happy enough.'

Elaine looked at him scornfully. 'No need to make up stories, Stan. I'm not interested, anyway.'

194

And it was true at the time she said it. The few days on her own at the hotel had been so peaceful, that she longed to continue to live like that, with nothing but her work to break up her days.

She appreciated having all her meals prepared for her, having all her spare time for herself with no housework, and only personal shopping to do. She bought herself some new clothes, and each evening, in the lounge of the hotel, she treated herself to a glass of sherry as she sat reading magazines.

Perhaps the knowledge that it couldn't last made Elaine more aware of the ease of this way of life, and still the tiredness persisted, leaving her reluctant to make plans for the future.

She caught a glimpse of Deborah one day. The girl was looking in a shop window on the other side of the road, and Elaine was waiting on the edge of the pavement to cross, before she realised what she was doing.

She drew back and watched her

daughter carefully, trying to see Deborah's face, to know that she was all right, not too unhappy. Then Deborah walked away quickly, and Elaine was glad to let her go.

Nevertheless, the solitary life eventually began to pall, and common sense took over. It was costing more each week to live than Elaine was earning, so she couldn't stay at the hotel much longer. She wondered if Rachel had had the solicitor's bill, and how it could be paid.

She began to worry again, and there was no longer any enjoyment in going to the theatre or to picture galleries alone.

She hardly dared to think of Andrew, for recollection brought to mind the expression in his eyes when she had left him. She hadn't believed Stan's story of the blonde, but perhaps Andrew had found someone — someone who was free to meet him and to marry him, to give him the love and comfort that he needed and deserved.

Elaine deliberately tormented herself with these suppositions, for she felt she had to face up to having lost Andrew.

He would never come back now — not after the way she had treated him. Besides, all the complications of her life still lay ahead of her.

Elaine wanted to ask Stan Davis whether he had seen Andrew again, but Stan regarded the whole affair as quite finished, as this was what he wanted. He had meant his jocular remarks about resenting Elaine being snatched away by a new husband. So he never mentioned Andrew now, and Elaine couldn't summon up the courage to enquire.

Then one evening, whilst Elaine was resting in her room, the hotel porter rang through to say that a gentleman was waiting to see her in the lounge. Her heart started to hammer, and she felt dizzy as she gazed at herself in the dressing table mirror. Hastily, she put on some lipstick and combed her hair. She noticed, for the first time, how hollow her cheeks had become, making her, she felt, look much older.

Andrew. Andrew had found her. She tried to steady herself before she started to walk downstairs.

As she came to the turn in the staircase, she looked over the banisters to see if she could see Andrew waiting for her. But there was no one resembling him. Only one figure waited. A slim young man, who stood with his back to the stairs.

Elaine moved on, feeling that a great stone had suddenly weighted her chest. When she reached the bottom step, she stopped. No. Andrew was nowhere to be seen.

The young man turned. 'Tim,' Elaine exclaimed. 'How did you know I was here?'

Tim gripped her hands. 'I had to find you. Deborah wanted me to. So I started a round of the hotels. Just on the off-chance. I felt sure you wouldn't have left the town. They'd enquired at your office, of course, but the man there would tell them nothing. Debbie was so worried.'

'Was she? Was she really?'

'Of course she was. You'd disappeared, and they never heard a word. They're miserable without you.'

Elaine sat down. 'I had to get away for a bit, Tim. I was at the end of my tether. I thought it might do them good to be on their own for a while.'

Tim sat beside her. 'They're in a mess. The house is dirty. They don't get any decent meals. And they're short of money. Debbie left the college and got herself a job, but, of course, she doesn't earn much. And Rachel's worried to death about the solicitor's charges. She had to ask if she could pay a bit at a time, but I got dad to lend her the money for it.'

'Oh, we can't let him do that.'

'Won't you come back, Elaine? They really do need you.'

She nodded slowly. 'It looks as if I shall have to. I want to, of course. It's a lonely life in an hotel, but, at least, it's given me a break. I'll go and pack. I shall have to go to the office tomorrow, then I'll go home afterwards — as I used to.'

Tim squeezed her hand gratefully. 'Good-oh. Let's go and celebrate, shall we?'

She looked round. 'We can get a drink here,' she said.

'No. Not this place. We want somewhere more lively. Besides, I promised to meet Debbie. Do come with me. It will make her happy.'

Elaine hesitated. 'Where have you promised to meet?'

'At the Dragon — or nearby.'

'The Dragon. Oh, that's the place . . . my boss sometimes goes there.'

'Don't you like it then?' Tim asked.

She smiled. 'It's all right.' She didn't say that she had heard that Andrew, too, went there, and that they might see him. 'I'll get a coat,' she said.

The Dragon was quiet when they arrived. A few people sat at the tables in the bar. Tim found an empty one, got

Elaine a drink, and asked to be excused. 'I said I'd meet Debbie at the end of the road. She doesn't like coming in here on her own.'

'I'm surprised you should bring her at all,' Elaine commented.

'I only let her have soft drinks,' Tim assured her, and again Elaine smiled at the confidence of this young man who could tell Deborah what to do.

He went off, and she sipped her drink slowly, to make it last out. More people came in, and the bar soon filled up. A man came over to Elaine, and asked if he could sit at her table. 'Everywhere else is taken up,' he said, standing with his glass of whisky in his hand.

She nodded her consent, and the man, who had a slack mouth and shifty eyes, sat down heavily, close to her. She edged away. The man started to talk, about the weather and the town. He must have had a lot to drink already, for his breath smelled of whisky, and sometimes he slurred his words.

He put out a hand and took one of Elaine's, which she snatched away. 'That's enough of small talk, little girl. Let's get down to it, shall we? Have you a place of your own?'

Elaine started to get up, but the man put an arm round her waist and held her down. 'Now, don't be coy, sweetie. Don't mess about.'

'Leave me alone,' Elaine hissed. 'I'm waiting for someone.'

'Now don't give me that.' The man's voice was loud, and Elaine felt that everyone could hear him. But the other customers were lost in their own conversations. 'We all know why ladies sit in pubs on their own. Waiting for someone? Well, that someone's me.'

Elaine pulled herself free, but the man hung on to her sleeve. 'Not so fast, pet. Where shall we go?'

Elaine managed to get to her feet, and the man unsteadily did the same, pulling on his overcoat. She pushed her way through the people standing between her and the door. She would find Tim.

Before she could get the door open, the man was beside her, grabbing her, trying to kiss her.

Elaine bit back a scream, and pushed at the man's chest to free herself, but his mouth clung, disgustingly, to hers. She was conscious of the door opening. She felt a hard hand on her arm, pulling her back, and a fist came smashing into the man's face.

He yelped and staggered, and people exclaimed and moved away, so that he wouldn't knock into them. Elaine glanced over her shoulder into the furious face of Andrew Nicholson.

The landlord came fussing around. 'Now what's all this. I don't want any bother here. Outside with you, if you can't behave.' He started pushing Andrew and Elaine out of the door.

'Fine company you keep,' Andrew exclaimed when they stood outside in the fresh air. Her words of thanks died on her lips.

The drunken man was propelled through the pub door. 'Here, you're not pinching my girl,' he yelled. 'I saw her first, didn't I honey?' He came at Andrew, arms flailing. Andrew hit out and the man was soon sprawling on the ground. Andrew grabbed him to pull him upright. 'Leave him. Leave him alone,' Elaine said. 'Do you want the police here?'

The man propped himself up against the wall. 'I damn well don't. You can keep the popsie,' he called to Andrew. 'None of 'em's worth fighting about. Ten a penny, they are. Ten a penny. Even snooty bitches like her.' He lurched away, and made his wavering way down the street.

'You'll perhaps be more careful in future,' Andrew said with ice in his voice. 'I'll take you to wherever you are staying. My car's in the car park.'

'No, thank you,' Elaine said in a matching tone. 'You evidently have the wrong impression.'

Andrew looked dubious.

Elaine's voice took a higher note. 'I

came here with Tim. He has gone to meet Deborah at the end of the road. She's late, as usual, I suppose.'

'Tim? How did he know where to find you?'

'He didn't. He came to my hotel, and we came here together.'

'I see. I'm glad I could be of assistance. Then you don't need me any more.' He moved away and started to cross the road.

'Andrew.' Elaine knew she had called him. He hesitated, half turned, and the car knocked him down.

She screamed. There was a hubbub of voices. People ran from all directions. Elaine pushed her way through them and knelt by the still figure on the road.

'Is he dead?' She didn't know whom she was asking. 'Is he dead?'

'I've rung for an ambulance, missus,' someone said.

The car driver was moving about, taking short, jerky steps. 'I couldn't help it. I couldn't help it,' he repeated, over and over again. 'If he hadn't turned . . . '

Elaine moaned. Again, she had unwittingly killed a man. This time it was the man she loved.

10

The ambulance came rapidly, shrieking its way through the traffic. White-coated men with kind hands and gruff voices, lifted Andrew Nicholson onto a stretcher and into the vehicle.

'Are you his wife?' one of them asked Elaine. She didn't reply, but stepped into the ambulance and sat on the end of the bench where the stretcher had been laid.

All the way to the hospital she stared at the white, inanimate face. She was gripped by icy terror.

Once at the hospital's casualty unit, the stretcher was taken away, and Elaine was pushed down on to a seat in the waiting room. Every time a nurse, or a white-coated man passed her, she asked the same question. 'Is he dead?' They all shook their heads at her, and she stayed still, paralysed by grief.

Andrew had once said that Elaine would have to choose whom she loved best — her daughter, or the man who had come into her life. Now she knew the answer. It wasn't a question of loving one more or less than the other, but there was one for whom she had the greatest need. It was so clear now. Why had she ever hesitated?

It was her vacillating that had led Andrew to his death. This time, she would die too. She couldn't go on living in the knowledge that she had, in her selfishness, brought his life to an end.

Deborah didn't need her mother any longer. She had Tim. Elaine had seen that in the young man's anxiety for herself. And Rachel — well, like so many other women, she would be left with her possessions and her memories.

Someone was gripping Elaine's shoulder. She looked up into the concerned face of a young doctor. 'Don't be so upset,' he said. 'Your husband's going to be all right. Some nasty concussion, and the usual bruising. We've put him to bed in Garner Ward. You can see him for a moment before you go.'

Relief seemed to ebb all Elaine's strength away. 'He'll be all right?' she asked, as though she couldn't believe it. 'I thought he was dead.'

'No. He seems pretty tough. But he's going to have a nasty headache for a bit. You'll have to hold his hand.'

Without being conscious of moving, Elaine followed the doctor to Garner Ward. Andrew, with a bandaged head, was in a bed near to the door. His eyes were closed, and she bent and kissed his eyelids softly, gently.

He opened his eyes and looked at her, but did not speak. Neither did she. She took his hand and stroked it, and she felt his grip on her fingers. She smiled down at him. 'It's going to be all right,' her eyes told him. Reassured, he closed his eyes again, and a nurse came to take Elaine away.

She went back to her hotel for one more night. She needed an interval for planning her happiness. Tomorrow, she would go home.

She went to work as usual, and rang from the office to the hospital to enquire about Andrew. A cool voice told her that he was 'comfortable'. She had to be content with that.

After the office closed, she went to see Andrew, and found Tim there. Andrew managed to smile at them both, but was still unable to talk.

'I'll take you home,' Tim said when visiting time was over. She folded herself into his shabby old car. Her suitcase had been put into his small boot. Soon they were outside Rachel Barrington's house, and Elaine saw her daughter's face peering through the front window.

She thanked Tim for the lift, and asked if he were coming into the house.

'Not just now,' he said. 'You'll have a lot to talk about. And don't worry about Deborah, Mrs. Barrington. I'll be taking care of her, you know.'

Elaine took his hand gratefully. 'She's

a lucky girl,' she said.

Elaine carried her case through the front door, and Rachel Barrington came into the hall. 'So you've decided to come back, have you?' The voice was unwelcoming.

'Yes, for a short time,' Elaine answered.

'What do you mean, for a short time?'

'I'll tell you later.'

There was a silence, and Deborah came out of the dining room, to stare accusingly at her mother. 'So it was true about you and . . . ' She burst into tears, and ran past her mother and her grandmother, to go upstairs.

'Now see what you've done,' Rachel exclaimed. 'I don't know why you bothered to come back.'

'To see that you are all right,' Elaine said evenly. Nothing could ruffle her now. She left her case in the hall, and went upstairs to talk to her daughter.

Deborah's bedroom door was unlocked. Elaine went in and sat on the edge of the bed, where Deborah had thrown herself. 'Come, love,' Elaine said. 'Let's try to be sensible.'

Deborah didn't answer, and Elaine started to talk quietly. 'I expect your pride is hurt. You imagined that Andrew was more than fond of you, when, all the time, his interest was paternal. But, Debbie, you'd be unusually lucky not to have at least one unhappy love affair, before you found the right person. We all do. It's good for us, really. It helps us to appreciate real love, when it comes along.'

Deborah had stopped crying and was listening. Elaine went on. 'That is what I have found with Andrew. It's somewhat late in life, isn't it? We need each other. I have you, I know, but very soon you'll be marrying and starting a separate life, which is natural and right. The generations must live within their own milieu, and the two shouldn't overlap.'

Deborah sat up, and as if she had not heard what Elaine had been saying, she asked, 'Why did you go away like that? Why did you leave us?'

'Because I was near to breaking point. I was torn between you. You — and Andrew. And the strain was getting too much for me. It was silly, I know.'

'I missed you,' Deborah said petulantly. 'It was awful here, with no one to do anything.'

Elaine sighed. Still the same selfish Deborah, putting her own comfort before all else. Well, Elaine had her share of blame for that, and it was doubtful if Deborah would alter very much, beyond mellowing somewhat as she grew older. Perhaps, with children of her own . . .

'How is Andrew?' Deborah cut in.

'All right. It will take time for him to get over the injuries. But he's going to be all right.'

'How will you tell gran about getting married? She won't like it.'

'Of course she won't. I was married to her son, and she's almost bound to regard my falling in love again as treason. But life is long, and one can't go on blaming oneself for ever . . . '

Deborah was silent for a moment. Then, with an effort. 'I know you weren't to blame for that accident, mum. I've felt, ever since you stood in for me about the car — I've felt I've been mean, unfair.'

'You needed a scapegoat, didn't you, Deborah? You had been crippled. Your father was dead. It was an overwhelming situation for a young girl. So you needed someone or something to blame. Well, if it helped you . . . '

Deborah got up and stood by her dressing table. 'Tim says he doesn't mind about my foot.'

'Of course he doesn't. He's always been fond of you, Deborah. I think you're perfect in his eyes.'

Deborah turned to her mother and regarded her solemnly. Then with some difficulty, she spoke. 'I hope you and Andrew will be very happy.' She turned abruptly away again.

Elaine felt the sting of tears, and longed to take her daughter in her arms, but she merely spoke quietly. 'Thank you, darling. I hope you will be, too.'

'I?' Deborah exclaimed. 'I haven't said I'll marry Tim yet. And we'll have to wait ages and ages. He has to get his degree, then a job before he has any money.'

'The waiting won't be too bad,' Elaine assured her. 'You must work, too. It mustn't be a one-sided affair. You will be going into it together.'

Deborah sighed. 'I suppose so. I think I love Tim. At least, I wouldn't like him to marry someone else. He wants to get engaged. What do you think?'

Elaine's spirit soared. Her daughter, who had despised and ignored her mother for so long, was actually asking for advice. 'You must decide, Deborah. If you don't want to be tied down, then wait until Tim's finished at University, then see how you feel. You have to be very sure.'

'Oh, I am,' Deborah said and smiled. 'But I don't want him to know how sure. Not yet, anyway.'

Elaine smiled ruefully. Deborah would never make things easy for anyone.

Elaine got up. 'I'd better tackle Rachel now. If she hears it from someone else, it will be worse than ever.'

'I'll come with you,' Deborah offered. 'I can twist gran round my little finger.'

'That's nothing to be proud of — playing on another's weakness,' Elaine protested.

Deborah shrugged. They went downstairs together. Rachel was in the sitting room. It was an indication of her state of mind that she hadn't switched on the television set.

'I suppose you expect to carry on as usual now,' she said as Elaine came into the room. 'Now you've had a bit of a fling, you think everything can be as before.'

'No, Rachel. Not at all. Things are going to be very different. I've come

216

back only until . . . until I am married again.'

Rachel's mouth dropped open. She pushed at the arms of her chair until she was on her feet. 'So you're going to do it. You're Michael's wife. How can you go to another man? How can you? And what about us? Me and Deborah? How can we live on our own?'

Elaine pushed her mother-in-law back into her chair. 'Now, please don't get so upset. You must have guessed it would happen. Michael has been dead for four years, and even when he was alive . . . '

'What. Are you going to smear his memory?'

'No, but you must know the truth. We weren't very happy together. If it hadn't been for Deborah, I would have left him long ago.'

'You wicked woman. You wicked woman,' Rachel wailed. 'He was good-ness itself, my son was. And you killed him. And now you have the nerve . . . '

'Be quiet, Grandma.' Deborah's voice

217

was sharp. 'Don't go on at mother like that. She isn't wicked. She never has been. And she didn't kill daddy. I did. I pulled at her arm and made the car swerve.'

'You. You, my baby? No. No, it's not true.' Rachel's eyes were wide with horror. She couldn't bear to hear Deborah taking the blame. 'You're talking wildly, my little love. You and your daddy, you both suffered because of her. Perhaps it's as well she's going. We'll never be truly content whilst she's here to remind us all the time.'

Deborah went to her grandmother and kissed her. 'Stop carrying on. It does you no good. It does nobody any good. Mum's going to be happy, and perhaps she deserves it.'

'And how shall we manage? Just us two, Deborah? Who will look after us? You know what it's been like these last few weeks.'

Elaine sat down. 'I shan't see you want for anything, Rachel. I will probably still work when I'm married to

Andrew, and from what I earn, I will give you enough to make sure of your comforts and for help in the house. I'll see that you don't suffer because of my going.'

Rachel sniffed, not to be conciliated. 'I think I'll go to bed. This has been a terrible shock for me. I still don't see how Debbie and I are to manage on our own.'

Elaine didn't speak again until Rachel had gone. 'I don't think I could ask Andrew to live here,' she said to Deborah. 'It wouldn't be fair — with Rachel so antagonistic.'

'No, don't bring him here,' Deborah answered. 'We'll fix something up. You'll see.'

'Rachel will have to resign herself to being entirely alone in due course. When you are married, Deborah.'

There was a quick knock on the front door, and it was opened immediately. Tim came into the sitting room.

'Could you bear to live with gran?'

Deborah demanded of him.

He hesitated. 'I suppose so. She's always been all right to me.'

'Good. Then that's settled.'

'Do you mean ... ?' Tim asked incredulously. 'That you've decided to marry me?'

Deborah put him off. 'Not decided. Just thinking about it.'

Tim grinned. He refused to be discouraged. 'Good-oh. Let's go out and celebrate.'

Elaine watched them go, warmth and contentment in her heart. The telephone rang. It was Andrew, telephoning from the trolley they had brought to his bedside.

'I had to speak to you, Elaine. Is everything going to be all right?'

'Absolutely all right, my darling. I've even settled with Rachel.'

'You're sure you love me enough to desert them — Deborah and Rachel?'

'I shan't desert them, Andrew. I couldn't. Besides, when I am so happy myself, I shall want to share it with them. I shall try to look after them — from afar.'

'So long as it's that,' Andrew said. 'Oh, Elaine. I can hardly believe it.' He gave a contented sigh, and rang off.

THE END

We do hope that you have enjoyed reading this large print book.

Did you know that all of our titles are available for purchase?

We publish a wide range of high quality large print books including:
Romances, Mysteries, Classics
General Fiction
Non Fiction and Westerns

Special interest titles available in large print are:
The Little Oxford Dictionary
Music Book, Song Book
Hymn Book, Service Book

Also available from us courtesy of Oxford University Press:
Young Readers' Dictionary
(large print edition)
Young Readers' Thesaurus
(large print edition)

For further information or a free brochure, please contact us at:
Ulverscroft Large Print Books Ltd.,
The Green, Bradgate Road, Anstey,
Leicester, LE7 7FU, England.
Tel: (00 44) **0116 236 4325**
Fax: (00 44) **0116 234 0205**

DUET IN LOW KEY

Doris Rae

In their quiet Highland village, the minister, David Sinclair, and his wife Morag, await the return of their daughter Bridget from convalescence. But a newcomer to the village causes Morag some consternation. Ledoux, big and flamboyant, is a Canadian forester, and has caused a stir locally. Morag fears that Ledoux, at a loose end in the quiet community, might make a play for their gentle and innocent daughter — and the potential for scandal would never do . . .

ONLY A DAY AWAY

Chrissie Loveday

When Sally is offered a position in New Zealand, she sees it as the opportunity of a lifetime. Unfortunately, her mother doesn't share her view — and neither does her fiancé. Sadly, she hands back his ring and looks to an uncertain future. When Adam arrives in her life though, along with a gorgeous little boy, everything becomes even more complicated. But New Zealand works its own brand of magic, and for Sally an unexpected, whole new life is beginning . . .

WHENEVER YOU ARE NEAR

Jeanrose Buczynski

After her break up from a disastrous engagement, Sienna Churchill is ready to make the most of life again and flies to Spain to work as a travel rep with a friend. However, six months later she returns home to her father's farm — and makes a shocking discovery when a ghost from the past reappears . . .

YESTERDAY'S SECRETS

Janet Thomas

Recently divorced archaeologist Jo Kingston comes home to Cornwall with her daughter Sophie to live with her father. When her old 'flame', Nick Angove, is injured on a dig Jo takes over, but faces fierce resentment from him. Then, intriguingly, human bones are found and the police become involved. Nick is injured, apparently when disobeying orders, but actually in saving Sophie's life. And as the truth emerges, they begin to acknowledge that their former love has never really died.